T0282159

AMONG WOLVES

BRIAN SHEA

KRISTI BELCAMINO

SEVERN RIVER PUBLISHING

1

Drake Martin blinked, trying to keep his focus on the blood dripping from his nose onto the concrete floor so he didn't pass out from the pain.

The red seemed abnormally bright, as if it were in technicolor, against the room's stark bleached floor.

Outside the raging wind whipped into a screeching frenzy every few minutes, rattling the wooden walls of the hunting shack and sending icy pricks of air through the cracks. Then he heard a sound that sent a shiver down his spine—the howling of wolves. He shook his head to clear it and the sound was gone.

The inside of the squat building, situated about a hundred miles northwest of Moscow, felt even colder than the arctic-blasted wildlands outside.

Movement in the shadows. Instinctively, he pulled at the restraints that bound him to the wooden chair, knowing it was futile, then braced himself for another swift punch or kick that would send more blood splattering across the floor.

But no blows came.

Beside him, Josh cleared his throat. Drake snuck a look at his colleague, who was also bound to a metal chair. Josh was unrecognizable. His face looked like raw ground beef seeping bloody juices and his eyeballs resembled runny eggs. Drake swallowed back bile that rose in his throat.

Keep quiet! Drake yelled inside his head. But it was too late.

"I'm an American citizen," Josh said through swollen, cracked lips. "You can't do this."

The words brought on a fresh attack—a deliberate, well-executed lashing with a thick metal chain. Fresh blood spurted from Josh's mouth, spraying more red on the floor in front of them.

Feeling as if he was betraying his colleague, Drake turned his head away. He couldn't help Josh. He couldn't even help himself.

Maybe they would have a shot if they had an inkling of what these Russian mobsters wanted, but so far, any pleas and questions had only sparked further beatings.

With his chin tucked down, Drake's eyes fell on his now shredded dress shirt. His wife had sent him the shirt a few weeks ago for Christmas. Even though he told her they could afford designer clothes now, he knew she still had scrimped and cut back on groceries for weeks to purchase the Christian Dior shirt that was now in tatters and stained with blood and other bodily fluids.

It was ruined.

She was going to kill him. He gave a strangled laugh at the absurdity of his thoughts, triggering a hard smack against his head that sent his vision reeling.

He heard the sound again—wolves howling.

He was losing it. It wouldn't be much longer before he simply gave up. He'd already offered to do anything the two men wanted, but they had kept eerily silent throughout the ordeal.

In fact, they hadn't said a word since yanking him and Josh from their vehicle just outside the walls of the Cryer Plastics Plant. The pair had been making a quick trip to the nearby village to appease complaints about dense smoke from the plant operations.

They had just rounded the corner from the compound's guard towers when two armed men jumped out of nowhere and held guns to them. The men had tied them up, gagged them, blindfolded them, and stuffed them in the backseat of their company-owned SUV before driving them to wherever this godforsaken room was located.

Once inside the frigid room, the gags and blindfolds had been removed and they'd been strapped to heavy metal chairs bolted to the floor. Without a word of explanation, the two mobsters had begun beating the two Cryer executives.

A bare lightbulb above them cast an interrogation-like circle of dim light that made it impossible for Drake to see much. That meant he could never anticipate a new beating. They always caught him off guard. Each time, when the mobster stepped forward into the light, it was as if a specter struck him and then retreated into the shadowy bowels of hell.

It took a few moments for Drake to realize that the two men had paused their attack for longer than usual.

He lifted his head and searched the darkness beyond the circle of light, narrowing his eyes but unable to see anything but shimmering shadows.

The pause was almost more frightening than the attacks. What were they gearing up for? An expectant silence fell across the room.

"What do you want?" he said, knowing that his words would provoke another attack but no longer caring.

It was inconceivable that he or Josh had anything these guys would want. They were brought to the Cryer Plastics Plant as pencil-pushing engineers who managed the plant while the CEO was out of town.

The wind started up again, and as it wailed, Drake heard something else.

This time he was certain—it was the howl of a wolf. Or several wolves. And it was growing closer.

Then the door to the hunting shack swung open and he watched the two rebel fighters walk out. The door slammed shut.

He turned to Josh.

"If you get out of here alive, tell Olivia I'm sorry I ever took this job. She was right—no amount of money is worth living here."

Josh gave a strangled laugh and then grew somber. "Tell my kids that I died with dignity. That I fought back to the very end. Maybe that I saved someone's life and died because of it. Just lie your butt off to make me look like a hero and not the coward I really am."

The sound of voices outside made them both grow silent. The door was flung open and a series of bright lights flickered on. As his eyes adjusted, Drake was paralyzed with fear at what he saw standing before him.

A huge caveman.

Drake shook his head to clear it.

Cavemen don't exist anymore, buddy.

But if they did, they would look like this man.

Drake tried to focus, blinking away the drops of blood slowly dripping from a cut above his left eyebrow.

Drake realized the man, dressed in a wolf-skin jacket, was flanked by two large wolves. He had to be hallucinating. He grimaced to hide an insane laugh bubbling in his throat. He knew what would happen if he allowed any sound to escape his lips.

Get it together.

Low, deadly growls filled the room. The two wolves stood thigh-high to the man, who was more than six feet tall and easily topped 250 pounds.

The lower portion of the man's face was covered in a thick beard and mustache. Above a bulbous, pockmarked nose, the man's eyes were dark glimmers of light peering out from thick black eyebrows.

Underneath the wolf-skin jacket, the man wore layers of brown camouflage clothing and what looked like a flak jacket. A massive yellow fang hung on a thick black cord around his neck, resting on his chest.

Out of the corner of his eye, Drake saw Josh emerge from his stupor and struggle to sit up. "What the? You're that guy on TV. That rebel warlord ... What's his name? Tiberius?"

Drake cringed, ready for the men to launch another attack on Josh for speaking, but instead the man in the wolf skin took a step closer. The wolves moved forward as well, keeping their noses close to the large man's thighs.

"Which one of you is in charge?" he growled.

Josh sat up straighter. "Him!" he yelled, blood-stained spittle flying everywhere as his head jerked toward Drake. "I'm nobody. You don't want me. He's the operations manager. I'm just a paper pusher. He's the one in charge."

His voice was frantic. One eye was swollen shut but the other was wild, bouncing back and forth between the warlord and Drake, who was suddenly very alert, watching the man in the wolf skin.

Tiberius leaned toward Josh. Slowly he opened his jacket and then turned sideways, pulling the collar away from his neck to reveal a jagged scar trailing from ear to neck to shoulder.

"That's ... that's a pretty nasty scar," Josh said, his voice shaking. He shot a wild look at Drake, pleading for help.

Drake tensed, knowing that it was only a matter of time before they were both dead.

Tiberius then took a step back from Josh. He stroked the fur of the wolf-skin jacket almost absentmindedly. "This is the wolf that marked me," he said. "He was a fierce warrior, a worthy opponent, but he was no match for my prowess. Now, he will be with me forever. Long past the days when the men who serve me and their bones are rotting in the ground."

"C-cool," Josh stuttered.

Tiberius frowned at the word.

Seeing the wolf man's face, Josh spoke quickly. "Like I said, I'm just a grunt worker around here. Drake here is the boss."

Tiberius nodded and Josh's entire body relaxed in relief. But Drake shook his head. Fool. Josh always was a little slow to read others.

Keeping his eyes on Josh, the rebel leader made a clicking sound and the wolves stood up straighter, their hackles raised, emitting low, rumbling growls.

"Wolf packs are very territorial. When another pack moves into the area, there is going to be a vicious fight. Your company has moved into my area," he said. "Do you know what that means?"

"You can be the alpha. I don't want to be the alpha," Josh said. "Drake's the alpha. You guys can have it out. Leave me out of it."

Tiberius blinked. "You're not in it."

Tiberius reached inside his shirt and withdrew a hammered silver whistle on a thick leather cord. He held it to his lips and let out a quick whistle.

Instantaneously, the two wolves launched themselves through the air and landed on Josh. They began to tear him apart. Blood and flesh flew everywhere. Josh screamed in agony as he was devoured alive.

Drake winced and closed his eyes to block out the horrors taking place inches away. He could feel the warmth of blood spatter and the impact of other larger, softer pieces hitting his face, neck, and head. It took all of his self-control not to panic. He knew it would be useless. He would be next.

He felt movement before him and opened his eyes.

Tiberius stood right in front of him.

"There can only be one alpha."

"I'm not the alpha," he said. "I'm just the guy in charge while the boss is gone."

The instant the words left his mouth, Drake knew he'd made a fatal mistake. He realized that the only reason he was still alive was that Tiberius thought he was the CEO of Cryer Plastics.

Now Tiberius would give the order for the wolves to kill him as well.

The big man reached for the whistle around his neck.

"Wait," Drake shouted. "You want the CEO? I can give you the CEO. He's heavily protected. I can get you to him."

Tiberius paused, holding the whistle near his thick lips.

"I want him now."

"I can get you in to see him. But if you kill me, you'll never get close. He's always guarded and the plant compound is heavily fortified. With me and Josh missing, they will clamp down even harder. You won't stand a chance. But I can show you how."

Drake spoke in a frantic rush of words.

Tiberius let go of the whistle and it fell back down to his chest.

"Continue," he said.

"I can show you how to get in," he said. "I can basically lead you to the man in charge. His name is Paxton Cryer. He's the owner."

Tiberius remained expressionless.

Drake knew he needed to up the ante. And he knew just how to do so.

"There's a safe in the compound," Drake said. "It has a rare diamond, worth a fortune." He paused dramatically. "And it also contains ten million dollars in cash. I can show you where the safe is."

Now he had Tiberius's attention.

"You will take me there," he said.

Drake nodded furiously.

Tiberius nodded at the two mobsters.

They reached over and cut the ties binding Drake to the chair with thick hunting knives.

Drake slumped to the floor and then crawled on his hands and knees like a skittering crab to follow Tiberius out of the open doorway.

The two wolves remained behind, feasting on Josh's body.

2

The streets of Barcelona were still wet with alcohol.

Despite the cool fall weather, thousands had flooded the streets with mugs of beer and bottles of wine, singing and dancing with arms looped as they gathered to celebrate the city's football team nabbing the championship win.

The energy had been building all day with thousands pouring into Barcelona to celebrate.

Once the championship was clinched, the city went wild.

Fireworks exploded off a footbridge near the National Palace, filling the air with smoke as thick as fog. Old furniture was dragged out of attics, piled high in courtyards, and set ablaze, creating massive bonfires that revelers gathered around to fight off the chill as they celebrated.

Even though it was near dawn, the Ramblas, the main pedestrian thoroughfare that stretched from Plaça de Catalunya square to Port Vell, still contained small pockets of carousers stumbling from bar to bar.

Off a main street, at a cafe tucked in an area near the Gothic cathedral, a different crowd had gathered around a small table—a well-worn professional arm-wrestling table with pads and nubs to grip to ensure a fair match.

A man with a blond crew cut and scruffy goatee was holding court at the table, crushing anyone who dared to arm-wrestle him. One after another, he took on drunken challengers. Each time he won he slid the cash over to his friend, a guy with a mohawk and ears that stuck out like handles. The sleeves were chopped off the mohawked man's black T-shirt, revealing arms covered in tattoos of pirates, ships, and skulls.

Unaware of the excitement in the back, Lucky, Shepherd, and Red strode in, chatting animatedly.

Full from a late dinner of paella, the trio decided to stop for a beer before heading back to bed on Uncle Max's yacht in the harbor.

Their entrance had garnered curious looks. Once they saw Shepherd's huge biceps and thick neck, the men eyed him warily, wondering if he was going to cause any trouble.

Standing a good five inches over six feet, Shepherd packed 260 pounds of nearly pure muscle on his frame. His muscular neck and well-shaped bald head were softened by warm brown eyes and a permanent sexy smirk. Now he flashed his grin at everyone in the bar, and it threw them off.

The locals barely noticed Red, who had an uncanny knack for blending in, fading into the scenery despite his distinctive blue eyes, bushy eyebrows, and shoulder-length gray hair. Something about his tanned, leathery face did make anyone who stood in his way back up a little bit as he strode through the bar.

After assessing Shepherd and skimming over Red, all eyes were on Lucky. When they saw her, they weren't quite sure what to think.

Unlike the vast majority of women in Barcelona dressed for Friday night on the town, Lucky wasn't wearing a slinky, provocative cocktail dress. Instead, she wore leather pants, thick-soled boots, a tight black T-shirt, and a NY Yankees cap pulled low over her eyes. With her curves, long silky hair, and flashing black eyes, they couldn't decide if she was the most beautiful woman in the bar or the most unpredictable one.

After ordering mugs of beer at the bar, the trio turned toward the crowd in the corner, which had just erupted in loud cheering and shouting.

"Regulars?" Red asked the bartender.

The man, who had a long, droopy mustache, shook his head. "Merchant marines. The two of them have been here since morning."

"Let's go see what all the fun's about," Shepherd said, jutting his chin at the crowd.

"I'm game," Lucky said.

Red shrugged. "Sure."

The man with the blond crew cut was taking a long pull on his beer when he saw the trio making their way through the crowd toward him. Watching them over the top of his mug, he kept his eyes trained on them as they grew closer. Then he put the mug down on the worn table, his lips curling up on one side in a sneer. He leaned over to the mohawked man and said something. Both men snickered.

Red swore softly under his breath, but Shepherd and Lucky didn't react.

Heads turned to see what the two men were looking at.

The man with the mohawk walked over and stood in front of Shepherd. Red and Lucky exchanged a look. The man had a jittery energy—the twitchiness of a drug addict. It was a dangerous aura. Shepherd remained relaxed and plastered an easy smile on his face.

"My friend, he wants to arm-wrestle you," the man said to Shepherd.

At those words, the crowd began to shout and cheer, and money was thrown down on a table as bets were placed.

Shepherd grinned. "Not tonight."

"Why not? You scared?" the man said.

"It's my night off," Shepherd said coolly.

The man with the crew cut now stood and spread his arms wide.

"Night off? This is not a job. This is not work. This is fun. This is how I relax."

"Maybe another time." Shepherd began to turn away when the man spoke in a loud voice.

"Maybe he is afraid to lose in front of his girlfriend."

"Girlfriend?" Shepherd asked.

Lucky burst out laughing and then brought her beer up to her mouth, taking a long sip.

Shepherd shook his head and started to head back toward the bar.

Lucky and Red followed.

The taunting grew louder.

"He doesn't want his girlfriend to see what a real man is like."

"Come here, honey, I'll show you what a real man is like."

"He is afraid. He is shaking in his boots."

The last one came from the crew-cut blond.

Shepherd stopped dead in his tracks.

He turned around.

The blond man grabbed his crotch and made an obscene gesture.

Red shook his head. "You don't want to do that."

"What, old man? Do what? Show the lady what a real man can do?"

The entire bar fell silent. The crowd parted, carving a path from the trio to the arm-wrestling table.

The silent room was tense.

A small smirk twisted the corner of his lips as Shepherd put his hand on Lucky's shoulder.

"I've got a better idea," he said, holding up his beer mug. "A hundred bucks says she'll have you pinned before I finish this beer."

The crowd burst into laughter.

The guy with the crew cut laughed, too, but only for a few seconds. Then his face grew still and serious. His friend with the mohawk laughed a little too long, far after the crowd had silenced. The first man shot his friend a deadly look.

Shepherd looked down at Lucky.

She shrugged. "Why not?"

As Lucky walked over, the crowd erupted in cheers and began throwing money down on a nearby table. Someone turned up the music. The throbs of AC/DC's "You Shook Me All Night Long" filled the air. The tables and bar stools emptied as everyone, including the bartender, crowded around. People were nodding their heads to the music, shouting, grinning, and waving money around.

In the middle of it all, Lucky stood calm, cool, and collected. Her black flashing eyes were focused on her opponent. Her poker face revealed nothing.

"I'm Flint," the blond said loudly over the music and cheering.

He held out his hand for her to shake. She ignored it.

"I'm Lucky."

His face creased as he tried to figure out if she was messing with him.

"She will pin me before you finish that beer in your hand?" Flint looked at Shepherd.

Shepherd raised the mug to his lips and took a sip before answering.

"Yup."

"How many minutes is that, you figure?" the blond asked the bartender.

"Let's say three minutes."

The merchant marine gave a loud guffaw.

"I've never had a match last longer than sixty seconds."

"There's always a first time," Red said.

"If she can even hold out for three minutes, I will kiss my friend Emir here on the lips."

The crowd jeered and hooted. The mohawked man scowled and shifted uncomfortably.

Flint looked around and smiled at the crowd.

"This will be fun. Let's do this. It looks like the big guy is thirsty."

With the bartender's help, Lucky got into position guided by the arm nubs and pads. The bartender did the same with Flint and then moved their hands together.

Her hand was tiny within Flint's beefy palm. Their elbows were on the pads. Their opposite hands gripped the nubs sticking up. They were locked and loaded.

But the bartender positioned and then re-positioned them. After holding their hands tightly for a few seconds, he released his grip and the match was on.

Almost immediately, Flint had yanked Lucky's arm to a 45-degree angle. Her arm was slowly growing closer to the worn wooden table.

Shepherd was at her right side. He took a sip and held the mug down where she could see it. The frothy foam was slowly disappearing.

Lucky's face was bright red and the muscles in her neck bulged as she strained against Flint's massive bicep threatening to shatter her hold.

Flint leaned slightly back and seemed to appear relaxed, but a thin sheen of perspiration was pooling at the top of his white-blond eyebrows.

There was no doubt that the merchant marine was superior in strength, but the match was lasting much longer than most people had anticipated.

It was clear to onlookers that Lucky wasn't trying to slam his arm to the wood, instead maintaining her grip like a dog unwilling to part with a bone.

Red smiled. He knew instantly that Lucky's play would be to outlast her opponent, wearing him out until she could make a move.

A skinny man with wire-framed glasses held up his phone and shouted out the time every minute.

"Two minutes."

The crowd cheered.

Lucky's eyes were hidden under the brim of her baseball cap.

Shepherd and Red exchanged a look.

If there was one thing Shepherd and Red knew Lucky was good at, it was being patient.

After all, she had patiently plotted and waited years to avenge her father's murder without the mere mention of it to anyone else.

She glanced at the mug in Shepherd's hand. The frothy foam was gone along with half the beer.

The view caused Lucky to grunt loudly and she readjusted her grip. Because her hand was so small, the readjustment instantly gave her leverage. She immediately twisted her hand so it was even more difficult for Flint to grip as tightly.

"How you doin'?" Lucky asked.

The blond frowned at her.

"Fine," he said.

"Looks like you're getting tired."

He didn't answer. Instead, he made a sound and regained his lost ground, pushing her arm back down toward the table.

Panting, Lucky closed her eyes for a second, her lips moving.

"You praying? It won't help you."

"You know what's interesting?" she asked. "Winning an arm-wrestling match has more to do with tendon strength than muscle size."

He scoffed.

"You know nothing about this. I arm-wrestle in different ports around the world. I know arm-wrestling. You know nothing. You are just a silly woman," he said with a sneer.

"A silly woman, huh?" Lucky exhaled deeply. Her voice was strained. "The reason you think you can win is because I'm a woman, right?"

He nodded. "It could not be more obvious."

"Do you arm-wrestle many women?"

"No." He frowned.

"I don't suppose you ever heard the name Irina Gladkaya."

"Who?" Flint grunted.

But Lucky had seen the flicker of recognition cross his face.

"Don't play dumb, Flint. It's not a good look for you. Being blond and all."

"She is an exception," he conceded.

Shepherd raised an eyebrow.

Red, who had been typing on his phone, handed it over to him.

"Thirteen-time world champion. Russian. Easy on the eyes, to boot," Shepherd read out loud before handing Red back the phone.

Lucky took the time to roll her eyes at Shepherd before returning her focus to Flint.

"I learned a few things from watching Irina," she said. "Namely, if your opponent is much stronger than you, wear them out a little first."

"First?"

"Ultimately, it boils down to this little trick."

"What little trick?"

As soon as he asked, she turned her palm toward her face and bent her wrist toward her shoulder.

Before he knew it, the movement had twisted his hand in the wrong direction and took his shoulder completely out of the match.

Lucky bore down on his arm with all her body weight.

"The push," she said, grunting. "Instead of the pull."

The crowd went wild as Flint's wrist grew closer to the table.

Lucky's face was now beet red. Her eyebrows were knit together and her jaw was clenched.

With a tremendous grunt that sounded like something between a scream of pain and victory, she slammed his wrist into the wood.

At that exact moment, Shepherd slammed his mug down on the table beside their hands. The bartender grabbed Lucky's hand and thrust it up into the air.

The bar was filled with cheering and shouting and the rustle of money being passed.

Shepherd laughed as he collected money and handed it to the bartender. "The next few rounds are on us," he said.

The trio began to walk toward the front of the bar. Red handed Lucky a beer. She chugged it as the crowd egged her on, not coming up for air until it was finished. Then she slammed the empty mug on a nearby table and wiped her mouth with her sleeve.

"I'm going to use the head," Red said, and disappeared toward the bathroom.

Lucky had just pulled out a bar stool to sit down when something crashed behind them. The bar grew silent.

They stopped and turned.

Flint had flipped the old arm-wrestling table onto its side and in four long strides had ended up a few feet away from them. His legs were spread and he was holding a knife.

His mohawked friend was with him. A narrow path led to them, flanked by high-top tables full of people. The mohawked man stood slightly behind Flint as there wasn't any more room. The merchant marines would have to come at them one by one.

"You have mocked me and disgraced me," Flint said to Lucky.

"She just beat you on the table," Shepherd said. "Don't make her beat you on the floor."

"It was a fair match," Lucky said calmly.

"The hell it was," Flint said.

"Listen, pal," Shepherd said. "Why don't you sit down and have a beer. On me."

The man with the mohawk lifted his shirt to reveal a gun. Two other men stepped in front of Flint and his friend. One had brass knuckles. The other held a switchblade.

"Looks like you're outnumbered," the man with the switchblade said. "We run as a pack. You mess with one of us, you get all four of us."

"Pity the four of you, then," Shepherd said.

Lucky slid off the bar stool and pulled her baseball hat down tighter.

"Let's get this over with, I'm ready for bed." She gave an exaggerated yawn, keeping her eyes focused on Flint, who was now standing behind the other three men.

"I'll follow your lead," Shepherd said in a low voice. "Keep them right in front of each other. We take them down one at a time."

"Just like in Istanbul," she said, nodding.

"Exactly."

With a roar, the man with the switchblade charged first, thrusting the knife in front of him. When he came within range, Lucky stepped to the opposite side and whirled into a drop kick that landed the heel of her boot on his neck. He tried to recover and swung at her with the knife, but she was now out of range on his other side.

Shepherd grabbed the man's forearm and twisted so the knife was now facing the man. Then he squeezed the man's arm so hard his grip on the knife slipped and it clattered to the floor.

Shepherd was now attacking the next man in line, the one with the brass knuckles.

The man swung and landed the brass knuckles right in the center of Shepherd's rock-hard chest. Shepherd glanced down at the man's fist for half a second before he threw a left hook into his right ear, sending the man flying to the side. Then Shepherd's right arm arced in an uppercut, catching the falling man under his jaw and sending him reeling back. But before he could fall back, Shepherd sent an overhand fist down on top of the man's head, sending him crashing to his knees. He was upright for a few seconds and then tipped over, knocking over several bar stools before he came to rest.

Lucky's focus was on the man with the mohawk standing in front of her. He gave an evil smile and lunged for her. As soon as he was within range, her boot landed squarely in his gut and sent him spiraling backward. As he fell back, she was on him, raining blows on the side of his head. He lifted his hands to defend himself and managed to put a few inches between them. It was enough for him to be able to reach down into the front of his pants for the gun. As soon as he had a grip, Lucky's hand was on his. Her elbow connected with his nose as her other hand broke the finger on the trigger, sending the gun clattering to the ground.

As he howled in pain, she grabbed his arm, twisted it, and then landed a kick alongside his ear, propelling his body into two tables. He collapsed and didn't get up again.

Now Flint stood in front of Shepherd, holding a large knife as they circled each other warily. Then Flint attacked, thrusting the blade toward Shepherd's neck. Shepherd blocked the attack and rammed his elbow into Flint's bicep, causing him to involuntarily drop his arm.

With the arm dropped and the knife out of range, Shepherd whirled and came down hard on Flint's wrist, causing him to drop the knife.

Before he could retreat again, Flint rounded and landed a powerful uppercut that sent Shepherd reeling and off balance.

As he tried to regain his footing, Flint kept coming at him, landing blows to Shepherd's jaw.

Seeing what was happening, Lucky launched herself at Flint.

Landing on his back, she immediately put him in a sleeper hold as

he violently tried to shake her off. Within seconds the man was uncon-
scious and Lucky leaped free as he began to fall.

A drunken bystander yelled, "Timber!" and everyone cleared a path
as Flint fell to the wooden floor.

"That's one for me," Lucky said, and wiped the sweat dripping off
her brow.

Shepherd made a face. "We're still keeping count?"

"Am I still breathing?"

He laughed.

They stood panting and looked around.

The four men were either knocked out or on the ground moaning.

"I'm done here if you are," she said.

"Yeah, I'm good," he said.

Just then Red walked back into the main room.

"What the hell is going on around here?" he said. "I can't leave you
two alone for a minute, can I?"

"That's right, buddy." Shepherd looped his arm around his friend's
neck. "Let's get you to bed. It's late."

"Yeah," Red said, and squinted. "I was just coming to round you two
up. I got a message from Max when I was in the bathroom. Vacation is
officially over."

Someone walked out the front door and the sound of wailing sirens
grew loud. Several people scrambled from their seats and rushed to the
door.

The bartender leaned over. "They don't like bar fights around here.
Or foreigners," he said, his voice low. "If you pass the bathroom door,
there's another door to a storeroom. Go through it to a door that leads
to the alley."

"Thanks, man," Red said.

The trio slipped out the storeroom door into the alley right when
squad cars pulled up in front of the bar.

As they headed down the wide, cobblestone pedestrian street
toward the harbor, Red's phone dinged with a text. He glanced down.

"Max?" Lucky asked.

"Nah. That gal I met in Sardinia."

"I liked her," Lucky said. "More than the woman you met in Nice."

"Yeah, me too," Red said. "I was going to see if we could head back over to Sardinia, but it looks like vacation is over. For now."

"It's been a good ride," Lucky said. "I don't think I've spent this much time off work in my entire life. You bozos sure know how to show a girl a good time."

Red laughed. "Of course you would think gambling, skeet shooting, and swimming with sharks is a good time."

He shot Shepherd a look. The larger man rolled his eyes and mumbled, "Don't get started, Red."

Lucky ignored the exchange. "Gambling is okay. Skeet shooting is a blast, and swimming with the sharks is—"

Red cut her off mid-sentence. "Shepherd, what do you think?"

"Want me to say it? Is that what it's going to take for you to lay off? Okay. Fine. I'm afraid of sharks. You happy now? You going to leave me alone now that I admitted it?"

Red laughed. "You are ex-Army Delta Force. As a mercenary, you've killed more people than I even want to know about. And yet—a fish is the thing you decide to be scared of? Fine. I'll leave you alone now."

"A fish?" Shepherd scoffed. "You mean an evil prehistoric soulless creature with beady black eyes that kills impudently?"

"A fish," Red repeated.

"Why do *you* like swimming with sharks, Lucky?" Shepherd asked.

She shrugged. "It's an adrenaline rush."

"What about their beady black eyes?"

"I don't really think about it. At least when I'm swimming with real sharks, I know what to expect. It's people who pretend not to be sharks that I have issues with."

"Speaking of sharks," Red said, "let's meet at sunrise."

"What do you mean, speaking of sharks?" Shepherd asked.

"What's the mission this time?" Lucky said.

"Protection gig," Red said. "Sounds simple enough."

Shepherd exhaled loudly and Lucky shook her head.

"I don't know about that," she said. "With Uncle Max, nothing is ever simple."

As they neared the yacht, an armed guard at the foot of the private dock nodded and unlocked the gate.

"Why don't you two catch a few hours of shut-eye and then we'll meet for a full briefing before we head to the airport," Red said as they boarded the yacht. "Pack warm clothes."

"I was getting used to having my wardrobe consist solely of bikinis."

"Same." Shepherd winked.

"Won't be any bikinis where we're headed," Red said.

3

Lucky sipped her espresso and squinted against the golden-orange glow that suffused the entire foredeck of the yacht. Red was talking to the steward and Shepherd was pouring his own coffee at a sidebar nearby.

After all three settled into their seats, Red took out a map and spread it on the table before them.

"Russia," Shepherd said. "I knew it."

Lucky made a face.

"Red said it was a protection detail so I wasn't looking at areas with unrest," she said in a defensive tone. "Besides, Shepherd, you said Kazakhstan."

"I was close."

"Close doesn't count."

"I was a lot closer than your guess—England."

"It's damn cold there. That's what I was thinking," she said. "I figured maybe Prince Andrew needed our protection after those photos showing him with Jeffrey Epstein."

Red laughed so hard he nearly spit out his coffee.

"I don't think Uncle Max and the prince are on speaking terms."

"Good thing," she said.

"But actually, Lucky, you are right about one thing," Red said.

"Oh yeah?"

"Your flight is to London. But just for a quick meetup and then you'll head over to Moscow."

"Meetup? With the protectee? He's English?" she said.

"Your protectee is the Shark," Red said.

Lucky let out a low whistle.

"And here I thought he was made up—like Bosley from *Charlie's Angels*, you know. Even when Max used to call me himself, he always spoke reverently about the Shark."

"The Shark?" Shepherd asked. "You've got to be kidding. Who is the Shark?"

"You haven't heard about the Shark?" Lucky asked. "He's like the mythical person in The Foundation who investigates all of Uncle Max's financials."

Shepherd frowned.

"The Shark's job is to unearth all the ways Uncle Max's money was used when he wasn't paying attention in the early years," Red said. "During some recent digging, the Shark found Max's investment in a Russian plastics recycling facility."

Red pointed to a walled compound surrounded by wasteland on the map.

"Cryer Plastics. Named after the CEO, Paxton Cryer," he said. "It's a plastics recycling plant, but when the Shark began to dig around, some of the financials didn't jibe and it looks like there's no real oversight. One of Max's advisors in the old days told him to invest in the company. Up until the Shark got involved, Max didn't even know about it. Now he just wants to make sure everything is above board since he basically funded the operation."

"What else is new?" Lucky said. "Uncle Max wants to be our modern-day Robin Hood."

"Except he's already the rich guy, not the thief," Shepherd said.

"Hey," Red said. "That's why we have jobs. If Max wasn't compelled to right all those wrongs, we'd be homeless bums."

"You might be." Shepherd took a sip of his coffee. "Not me."

Red ignored him and went on. "Seems that Cryer is old school. A lot of his financials are only documented on paper. No digital trail."

"How convenient," Shepherd said.

"The Shark wants to examine the books on-site and rectify the financial discrepancy."

"And if it can't be reconciled?" Shepherd asked.

"Max will make sure that his investment is being put to good use—one way or the other."

"As he does," Lucky said.

"The CEO appears to be cooperating," Red said. "He had planned to visit the plant this week and agreed to have the Shark travel with him and examine the files. Although Cryer has his own security detail, Max said he felt better if you two went along and watched out for the Shark since Cryer's detail is obviously going to focus on protecting him alone. And depending on what the Shark unearths, we don't want things to go sideways if we need to remove the CEO—hence your involvement. To complicate matters further, the entire region is destabilized and falling apart so that's another reason for you two to be involved. We'll join the Shark and Cryer in London and take another private jet to the border. That's where I'll leave you."

"I like all this talk about private jets," Shepherd said.

"Yeah," Lucky said. "After living on the yacht, I don't think I can handle flying coach. I'm used to top-of-the-line, state-of-the-art every-thing. Even toilet paper. Uncle Max has ruined me."

She and Shepherd exchanged a look and snickered.

"Then you'll like these high-tech wrist comms," Red said, opening a briefcase. "Your sat phones might not be reliable, and if you're captured and the phones are taken away, we've designed a special way for you to communicate with us."

He pulled out what looked like a piece of skin.

"It was first designed as a patch to deliver drugs into the blood-stream and quickly evolved into a way to hide a communications system. It's satellite-enabled and voice-activated and recognizable, but completely invisible," he said. "I've been wearing mine all day and you haven't noticed. Even if you're patted down, they're undetectable. A nurse could check your pulse and not even be aware of it."

He held up his right wrist. "I'll show you how to put them on."

Lucky reached for one of them. "Unbelievable."

"It's made of hundreds of thousands of nanostructures and numerous layers. It's being developed as a skin to put on robots. It's biocompatible with the elasticity of skin."

"Creepy," she said.

"Anything else we need to know?" Shepherd asked.

"Yeah," Lucky said. "These are cool and all, but you skipped over the 'if you're captured' part without an explanation. This must have to do with the region being destabilized?"

Red gave a long sigh and nodded.

"Yes and no. To complicate matters, it appears that the operations manager and the planning manager at the plant are AWOL. Nobody has been able to reach them for the past two days."

"What's that about?"

"Not sure," Red said. "The compound is heavily fortified. They disappeared after they left on a visit to a nearby village. You should familiarize yourself with the area. Your driver will be here in ten minutes."

Lucky and Shepherd examined the map and the satellite image printouts as they finished their coffee.

The massive plastics factory was enclosed within a walled compound. Two towers were perched on each side of the compound. A smaller building stood in front of the factory, facing the main gate.

"Are those guard towers?" Shepherd asked, putting his finger on raised structures along the wall.

"Like I said, the place is heavily fortified. It has its own security guard force and gun turrets in the towers," Red said.

"It looks like a prison," Lucky said.

"The walls around the compound are to keep people out—not in," Red said.

"You sure it's not a Gulag labor camp?" Shepherd quipped.

Red raised an eyebrow. "I'm not sure about anything except that Max isn't sending the Shark in alone, so that tells you something."

Lucky pulled the satellite image map toward herself and shook her head.

"This is the village those two were heading toward?"

Red nodded.

"This is the factory, obviously, but what are these two buildings?" she asked.

"The one on the left is where the employees live with their families," Red said. "That skyway connects it to the one on the right, which contains the CEO's living quarters and most of the offices."

Lucky blew out a puff of air and shook her head.

"Families? I can't believe anyone would willingly bring their families there."

"Must be worth it," Red said. "I'm sure for some people it's a huge opportunity—maybe a way to turn their life around."

As he spoke, the sun fully rose above the hills to the east and lit up the entire Port Vell.

"I guess," Lucky said, and looked around at the turquoise waters, the lush palm trees, and the golden sunshine. "I figure someone would have to be pretty desperate to willingly relocate their family to that wasteland."

4

An hour outside Moscow

Elizabeth Brody frowned as she looked around.

Rain pelted the already fogged-up windows of the bus. Pete Brody watched as his wife wiped off the window to see better. The only thing for miles around was a ramshackle three-sided structure with a tin roof and a rusted, dented metal bench inside. The shelter was surrounded by overgrown yellow grass that stretched as far as the eye could see.

"Are you sure we get off here?" she said, eyeing the bus driver.

She said something in Russian to him, but he just ignored her.

Pete knew his wife had been wary ever since the orange bus had pulled up at the Moscow airport.

So had the kids.

"That's not a bus," his daughter Cassidy had said. "That's a hippie van."

"Close, champ," Pete Brody had replied. "It's a 1957 PAZ-672 van."

When the kids boarded, Pete also pointed out in a low voice to Liz that not only were the 1950s vans commonly used as buses in rural Russia, but in some parts they also served as hearses.

"Keep that to yourself," Liz said.

Now his wife, who had been reluctant to get on the bus, didn't seem to want to get off. Pete stood waiting patiently beside his children.

"This is our transfer stop."

He watched as his wife's eyes widened. Her dirty-blond hair, which had been pulled back in a neat ponytail when they boarded the flight to Moscow yesterday, was now coming loose, and she had dark circles under her eyes.

In all the years they'd been married, Pete had never seen his wife look anything other than completely relaxed and chill. That was one thing that had attracted him to her in the first place: unlike the other girls at Ohio State, Elizabeth Barclay had always seemed self-assured. Her nonchalance was attractive and contagious.

It took a while for him to convince her to go on a date. But one night she finally agreed. He soon found she was kind, thoughtful, and funny. And loyal. She and her friends had been close since kindergarten.

He found out that her father was an extremely wealthy owner of a high-end grocery chain. In her hometown outside Columbus, her family had been known for their wealth. The best jobs in town were for her father's corporate office. Those jobs were coveted. Her father was a king in their small town—a domineering ruler who offered Pete a job soon after he and Elizabeth married.

But Pete had too much pride to work for his father-in-law. Luckily Liz agreed that it was better not to be under her father's thumb.

After working a steady job for a giant plastics company in Columbus, Pete had lost his job when the company went under. Unwilling to uproot his family, he had nearly lost their house while looking for work. He made it his full-time job, but openings were few and far between. Anytime he thought he had a chance, he was turned down for being overqualified.

During that rocky time, Pete and Elizabeth held firm and turned down several offers to work for her father's company, even when the foreclosure notices began to arrive. Elizabeth, who worked for a nonprofit charity supporting deaf children, remained optimistic and supportive, saying he would find something that would support their family.

An old friend of Elizabeth's finally offered Pete a night shift as a convenience store manager. Pete was grateful and worked twelve-hour night shifts, never seeing his family, when he got the final notice—they were losing the house. Nothing could be done. Just then, he'd been contacted by an old college buddy who told him about a job opportunity.

Within two weeks, Pete had been offered a job overseeing Cryer Plastics plant. The only hitch was that the job meant relocating to Russia.

Liz was reluctant at first.

"This is an amazing opportunity, Liz," he'd told her. "I am going to be number two in line at Cryer Plastics! That's huge. Normally I'd spend half my career working to get to that position. But they saw my experience and know I have it in me to do the job. It's a huge boon to us."

And the crazy thing was, he pointed out, Liz had been studying Russian because several of her clients at the deaf and hearing center were Russian immigrants, so she already knew a few words and phrases.

After they'd packed up all their belongings and put them in storage, Liz and the kids began to express misgivings.

"I want to be excited but what if the kids don't adjust well?" she'd asked.

"They're kids!" he said, and smiled. "That's why it's the perfect time to do this. Just think—all of us will naturally become fluent in Russian. That will be huge when they find jobs later on in life. This is an amazing opportunity."

After they'd landed at the Moscow airport and were waiting for their luggage, Liz had checked her phone. After seeing several messages from her father, she called him, worried.

"Where are you?" He had said it loud enough for Pete to hear.

"In Moscow."

Silence for a few seconds, then, "You're still at the airport?"

She looked around. "Uh, technically."

"Then it's not too late to change your mind. You know that Pete can basically take any job he wants at my company. I'm fine with that. I just want you to be able to maintain the lifestyle you've been accustomed to —or I should say the life you had before..."

"Daddy." Her voice held a warning.

Pete, who was keeping an eye on the luggage carousel, shot her a look. He'd heard every word. She rolled her eyes.

"All I'm saying is that it's not too late to change your mind. If he won't take my offer of help, at least you and the kids should stay home. You can come live in the guest house at the Hampton property."

"He needs to do this on his own, Daddy."

Now, an hour outside Moscow, Pete remembered this exchange and wondered for a split second if he was doing the right thing or just being a stubborn fool.

The bus driver was growing impatient. He turned in his seat to look at the Brody family.

"Come on, guys. This is the transfer station," Pete said.

Cassidy made a face. "This looks sketchy."

Pete looked at the man seated next to his son Will and shrugged. "Teenagers."

The man, wearing a square fur hat, remained expressionless.

"Come on, guys," Pete said. "This is where we catch the next bus."

Cassidy reluctantly shrugged on her backpack and scowled out the window.

Liz helped Will put on his backpack. He stood in the aisle and looked out the window.

"It's raining," he said. "We don't even have our umbrellas."

"It's okay, sport," Pete said. "We'll stand under that building until we catch the next bus."

"What if a bus doesn't come?" Will said. "I don't want to sleep here. I want to sleep in my own bed. I don't want to be in Russia. I want to be home."

Pete shot a glance at his wife over Will's head.

"Will," she said. "Remember what we talked about? How we're going to have a new adventure and learn to snowshoe and snowboard? You know how much you like the snow when we go visit Grandma."

Pete shot her a grateful look.

Will grumbled but didn't say anything.

"Let's go," Pete said.

After herding his family off the bus and running toward the shelter, Pete took out his phone.

"Any service?" Liz asked in a low voice.

He shook his head.

About thirty minutes out of Moscow, his phone had stopped working. He'd been trying to call the number he had for the factory, but it kept going to voicemail.

They waited two hours for the company driver before Pete received a cryptic text telling him which buses to catch to get to the factory.

Now, hearing her parents mention the phone, Cassidy's eyes grew wide.

"I knew it. We're going to die here."

"What?" Will shrieked.

"Don't listen to your sister," Liz said. "She's being dramatic."

The family quickly discovered that while the three-sided bus shelter was a place to get out of the rain, it offered little protection from the damp cold that seeped through their lightweight jackets.

"I'm cold," Will said. He gave an exaggerated shiver but his lips were slightly blue.

"You're right, sport, it's getting chilly," Pete said. "Let's get something warmer to put on."

He hoisted one of the four large suitcases onto the bench toward the back of the shelter.

"I think we have our winter coats in here," he said.

"Is that the one with Joey?" Will asked. "Can I have him now?"

"No, he's in the other suitcase, the gray one," Liz said. "Let's keep him safe there for now."

"Okay," he said.

Pete looked at his wife. "Why don't you look for the coats and I'll figure out where we are on the map."

"Good idea," she said. She began to rummage through the suitcase. "Here we go," she said, handing coats to the kids.

"But it's not even winter yet," Will said. "I hate that dumb coat."

"Me, too," Cassidy said. "Russia is stupid. It's not winter. It's only October."

"Remember," Pete said in a fake jovial voice as he shrugged on his own parka. "We'll get to make snowmen a lot earlier than we would if we were still in Ohio."

"I don't care," Will pouted. "What about Halloween? How am I going to wear my costume with this dumb coat on?"

"Hey," Pete said. "Let's look at the map and figure out where we are while we wait for the next bus."

"I'm sick of waiting," Will said.

Pete looked up. "I got an idea."

"Okay," Will said.

"Why don't you start walking in that direction toward Cryer Plastics." He pointed down the road. "If the bus comes before you get here, I'll do my special whistle like I used to do when you guys were little to call you home for lunch."

"Ha, ha, Dad." Will made a face. "Very funny."

"If you don't want to do that, I suppose you'll just have to wait for the bus with the rest of us."

Pete took out the map and held it against the back of the shelter.

"Is it going to be a real bus this time?" Will said. "That wasn't a bus. It was a van. And why were there chickens in cages on top?"

"They smelled," Cassidy said.

"It was the guy beside you," Will said. "That sandwich he was eating. I almost puked."

She was undaunted by her brother interrupting. "Do you think they'll have chickens on the next one or do we get a big bus?"

"Hey," Pete said. "Here's where we are on the map."

His finger trailed over to a different area.

"See, here's where we landed."

"Moscow?"

"Yep. And then we took a bus an hour to get to here," he said, tracing it with his finger. "And we're headed here."

"That's the middle of nowhere," Will said.

"It's about a hundred miles from the border," Pete said. "It's probably another hour on the bus to the factory and our new house."

"There isn't even a city near it. There's literally nothing there," Will said.

"Is it going to be nice? Our new house?" Cassidy asked.

"I think so," Pete said, avoiding his wife's eyes.

"You said the car picking us up was going to be nice, too, maybe even a limo, but it never came. What if the house is the same thing?"

Pete frowned.

"Well, I think something must've come up. But it's fun taking the bus. We get to see the land a little better and how people live."

"I don't want to see how people live. I want to be home. Not this home. Our old home," Cassidy said.

"Hey, look," Liz said.

A van was coming. It didn't slow down until the last second, splattering mud on them and stopping a car length past the shelter.

Pete held out his hand to his family.

"Wait here a sec while I check if this is our bus."

Holding his hand above his head in a futile attempt to protect himself from the downpour, he rushed to the passenger side of the van. The driver stared straight ahead. Pete tried the door handle. It was locked. He banged on the window. The driver turned and then rolled down the window.

Liz ran over and began to speak to the driver in Russian but he only looked at her blankly.

Then Pete spoke up. "Cryer Plastics?"

The man nodded.

"Okay."

The driver stared at him and then started to roll the window back up.

"Can you unlock the doors?"

The driver leaned over and hit a switch.

Pete ran back to his family.

"Leave the luggage here. Let's run through the rain to the van. You guys jump in and then I'll go get the luggage."

"Don't forget mine," Will said. "Remember it's got Joey in it."

Pete and Liz smiled. "Don't worry," he said. "I won't forget."

Herding his family toward the van, he yanked open the door and his family piled in.

The van was empty this time. The driver didn't move or say anything as they climbed inside.

Liz was searching for seatbelts and grumbling.

"There aren't seatbelts, Pete," she said under her breath.

Pete looked at her. He was outside in the rain, his hair dripping onto his face. "I'll be right back."

He returned with three of the suitcases, then opened the trunk and loaded them.

"That's all that will fit back here," he said. "I'll have to put the last suitcase up front with us."

He slammed the trunk and turned to get the fourth suitcase when the driver started to pull away.

Liz and the kids screamed. Pete ran alongside the van, yelling for the driver to stop.

"Daddy!" Cassidy shouted.

The driver realized what was happening and pulled back over.

Pete hauled the last suitcase into the van with him and plopped on the seat beside Liz.

She reached over and gripped his hand as if she was afraid to let go.

He gave her a grim look as water dripped from his wet hair onto the seat. The kids stared morosely out the windows.

An hour later, they pulled up to a giant walled compound with tall guard towers manned by armed soldiers.

The bus stopped in front of a set of massive gates near a guard shack. Above the gate the family could see two tall buildings connected by a bridge enclosed with glass. Glass staircases were visible on the outside of the buildings.

"What's that?" Cassidy's voice was filled with trepidation.

Pete squinted up. "A skyway, like we took when we were in Minneapolis to visit Aunt Mary."

"But that one is about a million stories high," Cassidy said. "There is no way I'm getting on that. Ever."

"Me neither," Will added. "I'm also not taking those stairs. What if the glass breaks or something?"

"Exactly," Cassidy said.

"Well, you go ahead and walk outside in the snow and cold but I'll be taking the skyway to get around."

"Whatever," she said. "You know that's not fair. You know I can't help it that I'm afraid of heights."

"She's right, Pete," Liz spoke up.

"I'm sorry, champ. I was trying to be funny. It was in poor taste."

Cassidy sniffed and rolled her eyes.

Two men wearing fur hats stepped out of the guardhouse carrying assault rifles slung over their shoulders.

"Cool," Will said.

Liz shot him a surprised look.

"They look badass. Look at those guns. Guess we aren't in Kansas anymore."

Pete rolled his eyes.

The guards were speaking to the driver as Pete watched and waited.

The driver got out and they frisked him.

"Oh my God, what are they doing?" Cassidy said. "This is like third-world crazy stuff."

Then a guard opened the van's sliding door. "Come," he said.

Cassidy shrank deeper into her seat. She reached over and grasped Will's hand.

Liz looked at Pete.

"Let's just do what they say,' he said in a low voice, then turned toward the guard.

"They're expecting me. I'm Pete Brody. This is my family."

"We weren't told to expect you," the guard said.

Pete's forehead crinkled. "They were actually supposed to pick us up at the airport and take us here, but I got a text telling me to take a bus."

The guard frowned.

"I know," Pete said. "It seemed odd to me too, but I'm the new head engineer here..."

The two guards exchanged a look.

"What?" Pete said.

"Come on," Liz said. "This is ridiculous. We've traveled halfway across the world. We are tired and hungry and wet and cold. Just call your superiors, they'll explain."

Pete plastered a big smile on his face and stretched out his hands. "Sorry, my wife is tired, it's been a long trip. But she's right, if you call the operations manager, I'm sure he'll explain."

Again, the guards exchanged a look.

"We can't do that," one said.

"I don't understand," Pete said.

"He's missing."

Pete's mouth was open now. "What? What do you mean missing?"

Liz stepped forward. "Then the other guy," she said, looking at Pete. "The other guy you spoke to."

"Drake. Yeah. I also spoke to him. Can you call him?"

The guard shook his head. "He's not available either."

Will burst into tears. "I have to go to the bathroom."

They ignored him.

"Okay, okay," Pete said. "Then I need to talk to Paxton Cryer."

"He's not—" One of the guards began to speak but the other cut him off.

"He'll be here shortly. He's on his way now."

5

As the private jet reached cruising altitude at 41,000 feet and six hundred mph, Lucky finished off her green smoothie and picked up a magazine. She pulled a thick cream cashmere blanket off the seat beside her and put it on her lap. The smoothie had made her cold.

The steward swooped in to take away her empty cup and hand her a bottle of water in its place.

After thanking the man, Lucky idly flipped through the magazine but quickly grew bored and threw it down on the white leather seat beside her.

Red was asleep in another seat nearby.

Shepherd was standing a few feet away doing bicep curls. The top of his head nearly touched the jet's ceiling.

After taking a swig of water, Lucky looked at him.

"What do you think the Shark is like?" she asked.

Shepherd exhaled and grunted his answer.

"He's a financial investigator, right? So skinny. Nerdy glasses. Long nose. Pointy chin. Your turn."

"Definitely glasses," she agreed. "But I'm going to go the opposite direction and say he's not skinny. Not obese, but not super thin, either.

Because he probably spends all his time at a desk poring over papers or sitting in a dark room full of computers and just eating junk food, you know. Too busy to actually go eat. And because he never leaves the dark room, he's also pale and has bad teeth—when you're really smart you're too busy to do basic things like eat and brush your teeth and go to the dentist."

"Like that goblin shark that lives at the bottom of the sea and has never seen the sun?" Shepherd asked, and flexed his left arm.

"Sure." Lucky put down her magazine to look over at him. "What's up with you and goblin sharks? Ever since that dive instructor told you about them off the coast of Morocco, you've been talking about them. You wouldn't even swim with the sharks that day. He told you they never come to the surface. They stay at the bottom of the ocean. It's not like they are going to come up four thousand feet just to bite your toes."

"They might." Shepherd gave her a side-eyed look. "How do you know they won't?"

Lucky rolled her eyes. "You've arm-wrestled an alligator, you've base-jumped from a radio tower, you've run through traffic on the autobahn to rescue a lost badger—and yet you are scared to death of a shark that lives at the bottom of the sea."

"Did you see the picture?" he said.

Lucky nodded. "They are pretty freaky-looking. So you're saying the Shark probably resembles a goblin shark? Really bad teeth. Beady little black eyes. Pale grayish skin. Slimy?"

"Exactly."

The pilot made an announcement for them to strap in for landing. Red grumbled but didn't open his eyes.

"Didn't we just take off?" Shepherd asked as he stored the dumbbells under a seat and sat down across from Lucky.

"It's only a hop, skip, and a jump when you're crossing Europe," she said.

As soon as Shepherd put on his seatbelt, he turned to Lucky.

"And the gums," he said. "Every time he smiles, you see about a foot of pinkish-gray gums."

He made a face.

"Okay," Lucky said, and ticked off the traits on her fingers. "Abominable snowman teeth. Dead eyes. Corpse-colored skin. Big gray gums. We should be able to recognize him right away."

"Let's make this fun," Shepherd said. "Whoever spots the Shark first owes the other person a hundred dollars."

"A hunny?" Lucky said.

"Yeah."

"You're on."

"This is such an easy gig we might as well make it interesting," he said.

"I agree. We're basically providing an escort service," she said.

"Did you just call yourself an escort?" Shepherd laughed.

"I called us both escorts," she said. "Besides, that's a big assumption. How do you know the Shark isn't into guys?"

He shrugged. "You're right. I guess I don't," he said. "Any way you look at it, this sounds like the easiest gig we've ever had."

"Maybe Uncle Max is getting soft," she said.

"I get that he wants his prized possession escorted into an area that is destabilized," Shepherd said. "That makes sense."

"Total sense," Lucky agreed. "But really he's paying us to be glorified babysitters."

Red grumbled in his sleep and they both laughed.

A few minutes later, the pilot announced they were making their approach to Heathrow Airport.

They both grew quiet and looked out the window.

Within seconds, the sunny day disappeared and they were plunged into thick gray clouds.

"I could never live here," Lucky said.

"I love the gray and rain," Shepherd said.

She rolled her eyes. "Of course you do."

"I've only been to Moscow once," he said. "A long time ago. I wonder if it's changed."

"It's probably still as screwed up as the last time you were there," she said.

"Actually, you're right," he said. "It sounds like it's getting bad again."

"Hence our assignment."

Right before the plane landed, Shepherd said, "I hope they at least have some good borscht where we're staying."

Lucky burst into laughter. "Borscht! Ha! You've never had that in your life!"

"I have!"

"Have not!"

Red woke up, yawning and stretching as the plane landed. "Best naps in the world are on airplanes."

"If you say so," Lucky said. "Has Shepherd ever had borscht?"

"Am I supposed to know everything about him?" Red asked.

"Maybe."

As he stood up, Red winced. Lucky was immediately at his side. "You okay?"

He nodded. "I'm good. The funny thing is, those gunshot wounds take longer to heal the older you get. It's kind of a rip-off."

"How many times have you been shot now anyway, Red?" Shepherd asked.

"Well, let me see." He grinned. "First time was in the Gulf."

Red was still counting off all the times he'd been shot when they stepped out of the plane into the blinding gray light of London.

They walked down the stairs onto the tarmac, where they were each handed a large duffel bag. A man in a white uniform escorted the trio to an area near another private jet. The stairs were down on this jet but nobody was around.

"Wait here," the man said, then got into a little cart and drove away.

Lucky pulled on some dark sunglasses and Shepherd followed suit.

"What now?" Shepherd asked.

"We wait," Red said.

A few minutes later, the airport door opened and a group of people stepped outside.

The first was a petite woman with black hair pulled tightly into a bun. She wore a navy blazer and matching pants and had black stiletto pumps. She was carrying a briefcase. On one side of her was a short, skinny man in an ill-fitting gray suit who kept pushing his glasses back up on his nose. On her other side, a heavyset, balding man in a dark suit carried a suitcase and wore sunglasses despite the gray day.

As the three emerged from the doorway, Shepherd said, "Gray suit."

"Black suit," Lucky said out of the corner of her mouth.

"Huh?" Red said.

"We're betting on which one is the Shark. Don't say anything."

Red burst into laughter. "Oh, I won't."

As the three grew closer, the woman moved to the front. The two men stayed half a step back. When she was a few feet away, she stuck out her hand. Red stepped up to greet her.

"Nice to see you, Red," she said.

Shepherd made a sputtering sound, which the woman ignored. She turned to Lucky first.

"Courtney Mako," she said.

Lucky broke into a huge grin as she stepped forward to shake the other woman's hand. "Evelyn Rodriguez-Toscani. My friends call me Lucky."

The woman gave a slight nod before turning to Shepherd.

"Adam Shepherd," he said, and stuck out his hand.

As Mako shook his hand, she said lightly, "You seemed surprised when I first walked up. Did you assume I was a man?"

"We both did," Lucky said in an apologetic tone.

"I'm actually thrilled that the Shark is a woman," Shepherd said awkwardly.

"The Shark?" Mako cocked her head slightly.

Shepherd and Lucky exchanged a glance.

Mako gave a wry grin.

"I'm joking. I know they call me that."

She glanced at her watch.

"I'm expecting Mr. Cryer any minute. As soon as he arrives, we'll board."

Almost as soon as she finished speaking, her phone buzzed.

She briefly glanced down at the screen and then turned toward the jet.

"Change of plans. We leave now."

"What about Cryer?" Red asked.

A delicate shrug.

"Apparently, he's already there."

6

Moscow

As the black SUV with the tinted windows and bulletproof glass merged onto the M-11 freeway heading north from the Sheremetyevo International Airport, the driver punched the accelerator so that the passengers were pressed back into their seats.

Once he regained his composure in the back seat, Michael Lockwood, a forty-year-old American man with a neatly trimmed brown beard and tortoise-shell glasses that matched his full head of hair, turned to look behind them. No one seemed to be following them so he turned back around. The mercenary behind the wheel met his eyes and gave the slightest nod.

Lockwood wasn't questioning the guy's ability to keep them safe, he just needed to see for himself. Already prone to nervousness, he'd been jittery ever since he received news of the kidnappings.

Tiberius, the rebel warlord, had broken the rules of the game and bit the hand that fed him by kidnapping two Cryer Plastics employees.

So far, they had managed to keep the rebel leader at bay with monthly payments, but now he wanted more. He wanted Cryer Plastics for himself.

He needed a company that size to launder his drug money. An American company was even better. He'd recently set his sights on the plastics factory.

He'd been pressuring Paxton Cryer, the CEO, to sell.

This latest move—the kidnappings—was pure intimidation.

Paxton Cryer, on the other hand, seemed more interested than ever in his Russian company since he'd heard news of the country's destabilization. He'd never said it aloud to Lockwood, but Cryer was clearly set on becoming another insanely rich Russian oligarch when the country went to hell.

The CEO and owner was a short, stubby man who thought expensive alcohol and contraband cigars signaled the height of sophistication. Right now his round face was uncharacteristically red and sweaty from the exertion of hustling through the Russian airport and being shoved into the backseat of the SUV out front.

The rich CEO wasn't used to moving fast and most definitely wasn't used to being ordered around, but the twin mercenary bodyguards Lockwood had hired wouldn't take no for an answer. They'd swooped in as soon as Lockwood and Cryer had stepped past security and marched them straight out to the waiting SUV.

Lockwood was glad for the protection he'd hired, but he thought the bodyguards were a little too movie-star handsome to really be assassins.

Although they dressed the part, in fatigues and combat boots, the brothers also had longish wavy hair, grizzly goatees, and disconcertingly green eyes.

They had been the most expensive bodyguards Lockwood could find on the darknet. Cryer had told him that price wasn't an issue, and Lockwood had agreed. They were doing business in a volatile country. You could never be too careful. Especially now that Tiberius had gone against their agreement. They paid him a small fortune every month to leave them alone. That deal was apparently off.

To make matters worse, that monthly bribe had triggered the interest of a majority shareholder who was sending an auditor to investigate. It was an utter shitshow.

"You going to introduce me to these fine young fellas in the front seat?" Cryer said now. There had been no time for small talk in the rush through the airport.

"Mr. Cryer," Lockwood said, adopting a formal tone. "These are the Darcy brothers—Clint and Connor. They're our protection detail during your stay. Now that our friend Tiberius is playing hardball, we will make sure they stay at your side at all times."

The driver met Cryer's eyes in the rearview mirror and gave a nod.

The brother in the passenger seat turned all the way around and grinned, flashing a perfect set of white teeth.

"At your service, sir," he said.

Cryer didn't speak but nodded and settled back in his seat.

Lockwood eyed the M4 Commando assault rifle resting casually on the lap of the man in the passenger seat. He knew another identical weapon rested on the seat between the brothers. Having the weapons a few feet away made Lockwood nervous. But the Darcy brothers were expensive, so they obviously knew what they were doing.

"Turn up the heat on these seats, boys," Cryer said from the back-seat. "What's this thing equivalent to? Like a Range Rover?" He looked at Lockwood.

"The Komendant is made by Aurus, the same company that makes Putin's limousines. I took the liberty of buying one with bulletproof glass and reinforced door panels. With everything going on..."

"Great, perfect. Excellent. That's why I hired you, Lockwood, to take care of details like that."

Lockwood leaned down and picked up a black case, setting it on the seat between them. He popped it open and revealed a portable mini bar. It contained a chilled bottle of Iordanov vodka and two chilled crystal-cut whiskey glasses.

Cryer nodded his approval.

"The Pamela Anderson special edition. Just as you requested."

"Those real Swarovski crystals?"

"Yes."

Cryer picked up the bottle and examined it. A large skull formed out of purple crystals adorned the front of the bottle.

"Next time get a more manly color. I don't like fairy colors like purple on my vodka bottles."

Next time don't ask me to try to find Canadian vodka in Russia.

But Lockwood kept his mouth closed and poured three fingers of the icy liquid.

The two men sipped the alcohol and then sat in silence for a few seconds.

"Should we talk about the, er, situation at the compound?" Lockwood said, glancing at the two men in the front.

"Sure," Cryer said. "Why not?"

Lockwood found his employer's nonchalance a little unnerving.

"If he thinks I'm going to sell because he is a bully and kidnapped one of my employees, he's out of his mind."

"He's definitely out of his mind," Lockwood said.

Then Lockwood pulled a leather briefcase onto his lap and took out a sheaf of papers.

"Let's go over your itinerary and the details of your stay," he said.

"My itinerary is for you to get our man back to get the media off my case and then for me to get my personal effects and get the hell out of here," Cryer said.

"Yes, but it might be more complicated than that," Lockwood cautioned.

"We expecting any trouble with this deal?" Cryer shot a wary glance at the brothers. "He should know not to screw with us. We need to get this handled right away. Someone leaked word about the kidnapping. I had calls from three journalists this morning. I can only put them off for so long."

"I don't anticipate any trouble. We meet, find out what he wants—"

"He's going to want money," Cryer interrupted. "The only reason he has any leverage at all is because the press knows about the kidnapping now. Who do you think did that?"

"It appears that your personal assistant, Wilson, called family members to let them know what was going on, and the family members grew concerned and contacted their senators."

"That is unacceptable. Fire the man immediately."

"Yes," Lockwood said agreeably.

"Actually, wait until I clean out my, uh, things, at the compound and am heading back home. Then fire him."

"Yes, sir."

"I can't believe he would take even one of our men—never mind two of them. And he has some nerve asking for anything now, after all we've done for him. If he thinks we're going to sell to him, he's got another thing coming. That's why we paid him all that money—to keep him off our back."

As he said this, Lockwood noticed the driver's eyes flash in the rearview mirror and then quickly look away.

Cryer didn't miss a beat.

"We trust these guys?" He jutted his chin toward the front seat.

"I vetted them. They are the best of the best. You need a top-notch security team in case things go sideways on this deal. We can't count on a Russian mobster to keep his word. We can only hope."

"What makes them so good, anyway? They look like slackers. Pot heads."

Lockwood lowered his voice and leaned over. "They're Omaha kids who were in Special Forces and didn't like what they saw there. They went AWOL, joined the French Foreign Legion, came out with brand-new identities. They don't really exist."

"Huh?" Cryer said. "No social security cards or anything?"

"Nothing like that. Invisible, basically."

"So you two are identical, huh?" Cryer leaned forward. "I bet you can really fool the women. Pretend to be each other and sleep with each other's girlfriends and so forth. Get way more action that way, I bet."

"We don't do girlfriends." The driver's eyes met Cryer's in the rearview mirror. "Too many beautiful women to sample, if you know what I mean."

"Well, marriage never stopped me from sampling, but I hear what you're saying," Cryer said, and sat back. "Take my advice. Stay single. I've got three ex-wives who are still trying to take me for every penny I've got.

Good thing I was smart and didn't let them know everything I owned or I'd be penniless right now. I've had to hide things from them. That's part of why I'm here and why I hired you two. I've got a few priceless objects to get back to the US. I'm going to need your help with that, fellas."

"Whatever you need, man," one of the brothers said.

Cryer frowned at the use of the word "man."

"I plan to clear everything out on this trip—and that means the safe," he said in a low voice. "I don't intend to come back here. Ever. I need to transport everything safely back to America. If anyone got wind of what I'm transporting..."

"You can trust these two men," Lockwood said.

"You better be right," he said. "If the right people knew what I have stashed in that safe..."

He trailed off and tipped back the last of the vodka in his Riedel glass before he looked out the window. The pane was streaked with raindrops.

"What the hell?" he said. "Look at that. A bus stop in the middle of godforsaken nowhere Russia. That tin roof looks like it would blow away in a breeze. How old do you think that thing is? Why would anyone be taking a bus out here?"

He swiveled his head in all directions.

"There's not a goddamn place around here for as far as the eye can see."

Lockwood shrugged and shuffled some papers.

"We can't wait around all day," Cryer said. "I need to resolve this hiccup and get out of here. When's the meet supposed to take place?"

"Today," Lockwood said. "You can deal with the auditor and I'll go see what Tiberius wants in exchange for our man."

"The auditor," Cryer said. "Don't even mention her. The whole situation is ridiculous."

"I think I came up with a way to explain the monthly payments to Tiberius," Lockwood said.

"How did she even become aware of the discrepancies?"

"Your former bookkeeper."

"Well, all that is over now," Cryer said. "Tiberius ruined that. Ruined it big time. Do we have assurances? Is our man even still alive?"

"I haven't heard otherwise," Lockwood said. "I'll ask for proof of life when I meet with him."

Cryer frowned. "I don't want him to think he's got the upper hand here. He may be a Russian warlord, but I'm nobody to trifle with."

"We're meeting him on his turf. It's going to be risky no matter what. We can't trust this guy."

"I know," Cryer said. "That's why I asked you to find someone like these two." He pointed toward the Darcy brothers. "You did good. I'll let you borrow them during the meeting with Tiberius. They should be able to keep you safe."

"Yes, they should." Lockwood bowed his head.

"What do I have planned after meeting with that nosy investigator?"

"We should arrive at the plant within the hour. You will meet with the auditor—her name is Courtney Mako—for the next two hours. That should give her enough time to look through the books. They've been adjusted to explain the payments so no worries there. Then you'll have time to take a shower and get a massage—I've got your regular girl lined up—before your meet-and-greet dinner with Peter Brody and his family. Then you'll have private time with Nadia. She arrived earlier today."

Cryer's eyebrows drew together and he cocked his head.

"I don't have time for her."

"She will want to be paid anyway."

"I don't care. She doesn't get a dime. If she doesn't like it, too bad."

"Very well."

"This meet-and-greet? Remind me who it's with again? Why on earth would anyone bring his family here, right now? If I were still married, I'd make sure my wife stayed on my Montana ranch. I could make conjugal visits every month, you know?"

Lockwood cleared his throat before answering.

"Yes, your ranch is pretty spectacular."

"Who is this fellow again?"

"Peter Brody. The new engineer."

"Ah, yes," Cryer said, "the new blood."

7

Russia-Poland Border

"Things just got a little more complicated," Courtney Mako said from the backseat of the SUV.

"What's up?" asked Red, who was driving. Lucky was shotgun. Mako and Shepherd were in the back.

"International media is reporting that at least one employee, possibly two, have gone missing at the Cryer Plastics plant in Russia. They are saying that family members reported being unable to reach the two men a few days ago. The CEO, Paxton Cryer, has been unavailable for comment."

"I'll check with Uncle Max," Red said, "but I'm pretty sure your protection detail is going to include figuring out what happened to those two employees."

"Cryer unavailable for comment?" Shepherd said. "Think that's why he ditched us in London?"

"Probs," Lucky said. "Can I turn up the heat?"

She shivered, leaned over, and flicked a knob before anyone answered. "My body thinks it's still on a Mediterranean beach somewhere."

"This is nothing," Mako said. "It is supposed to storm tonight. A whiteout blizzard. But we'll be safely ensconced in the Cryer Plastics compound."

"As long as we get across the border," Red grumbled. "Look."

As the SUV rounded a corner, they were greeted by a long line of cars snaking along the two-lane road. At the checkpoint, two tall guard towers flanked the tree-lined road. The towers were connected by a footbridge. On the ground, an enclosed tunnel formed by a chain link fence served as a pedestrian crossing. Both sides of the road were blocked by lowered traffic arms with large white and black signs saying "Stop" in English and Russian. A guard shack was nestled along the western portion of the road.

As the road grew closer to the checkpoint, black and yellow concrete pillars separated the opposing traffic lanes.

Lucky and Shepherd scouted out the situation with binoculars.

"Two men in each guard tower," she said.

"Looks like a machine gun turret," Shepherd observed.

"We got a guard shack ground level to the west," Lucky said. "Everyone is dressed in fatigues and heavily armed. They aren't messing around."

"This is Russia," Mako said archly.

Everyone ignored her.

Shepherd squinted through his binoculars. "In addition to those four guards, there are two uniforms approaching vehicles and examining documents. Looks like one is sweeping the vehicles for bombs while the other checks papers."

"They get many suicide bombers in these parts?" Lucky asked.

Red shrugged. "Wouldn't doubt it."

The vehicles in front of them scooted forward slowly.

Red reached for Lucky's binoculars. "You mind?"

He squinted for a few seconds and then handed them back to her.

"Is there a problem?" she asked.

"Not sure. I don't see your driver on the other side," he said. "He was supposed to be here already. You're supposed to walk through the checkpoint and get picked up over there."

"What's plan B?" Mako asked.

"I drive us all through and we wait in the vehicle until he arrives," Red said. "I'm not sending you in there on foot without a ride. I wasn't planning on crossing the border, but it's all good. I can easily come back across. It's not like they'll have forgotten about me."

The cars continued to creep forward until their SUV was at the front of the checkpoint. Two men in fatigues stepped in front of them and pointed their assault rifles at the windshield.

"Guess they want to make sure we aren't going to try any funny business," Red said.

While one of the guards remained standing in front of the SUV with his weapon pointed at them, the other came around to the driver's side window.

He grunted something in Russian and Red handed him everyone's documents. The guard stepped away and flipped through them in an agonizingly slow manner. He opened a passport, then looked inside the vehicle and matched it with other paperwork.

After going through all four passports, he did it again.

Then he frowned.

"Who's the chucklehead in the wanted poster?" Shepherd pointed to a giant flyer tacked to the bottom of a large blue and yellow sign with Russian writing.

"Tiberius," Mako said. "He's somewhat of a warlord around here. Controls the rebels."

"He's rocking the Chewbacca look with that hair and beard and fur," Lucky said.

"Those are wolf skins."

"Those poor animals," she said.

While they were speaking, the checkpoint guard with their documents suddenly shouted something. Two guards ran out of the shack with weapons drawn.

"What the?" Lucky said.

"Be cool," Red said, eyes narrowing and knuckles turning white on the steering wheel.

One of the guards headed toward the driver's side door and began to shout.

"He wants us to get out of the vehicle. Right now," Mako said, translating and reaching for her seatbelt release.

"Is that a good idea?" Lucky said.

"We don't have a choice," Red said, and jutted his head. Three of the guards had now surrounded the SUV.

"I'll talk to them," Mako said.

"For some reason I don't find that reassuring," Lucky said.

"You'd rather fight it out?" Mako sneered. "I know your type, you're all about brawn over brains."

"You don't know me," Lucky said flatly.

"Out! Now!" one guard said, waving the gun.

The four piled out with their hands in the air.

"Over here," the guard from the shack said in broken English.

He pointed with his gun to a spot beside the SUV.

"I don't fancy dying at a checkpoint in Russia," Red said.

"You don't have to worry about that, my friend," Shepherd said. "We've just got to figure out what the problem is."

"Mako's handling it." Lucky stood facing the guards, eyes focused on their every move.

Reeling off some clipped words in Russian, Mako was also gesturing madly, pointing at herself and the others and their vehicle.

The guard frowned and shook his head.

Whatever she was saying, he wasn't buying it.

She reached for her purse, and he shouted and pointed his gun at her. The other guard rushed forward.

The line of cars behind them was growing longer.

Quickly putting her hands up, Mako spoke in a flurry of Russian.

The guard lowered the barrel of his weapon and nodded.

Mako slowly stuck her hand into her purse and withdrew her phone. She pressed a few buttons and then held it up. The guard grew closer and squinted as he looked at the screen. He stared for a few seconds and then backed off. He turned to the other guard and said something. That guard lowered his weapon as well. The two guards moved together, speaking quietly.

Mako dialed a number and then turned her back to the guards as she spoke in a low voice.

After a few seconds, she put her phone back in her purse and turned around. She faced the guards with her arms crossed and foot tapping.

"What do you think she's doing?" Shepherd said.

Lucky shrugged. "Beats me."

The seconds passed. Everyone waited.

A ringing phone could be heard coming from the guard tower.

One of the guards was visible through the window holding a phone receiver. Then he hung up and shouted something to his companions.

The guard closest to Mako blanched. He said something to the other guard and the two headed back to their shacks. The checkpoint guards also stepped aside and waved the group forward, even though they were still standing outside the vehicle.

Mako turned and headed back toward the SUV.

"Let's go," she said, then turned to Lucky. "I guess brains over brawn wins the day."

Lucky scowled.

"Who did you call?" Shepherd asked.

"Who do you think?"

"Never underestimate Uncle Max's reach," Lucky said.

"Or his deep pockets," Red said, and turned to get back in the driver's seat.

The guards backed off, and Lucky had her hand on the door when machine gun fire erupted.

"Take cover!" Shepherd shouted.

The four ducked behind the SUV. Lucky and Shepherd swarmed Mako and shoved her to the ground near the SUV's front tire.

"Doors don't stop bullets," Lucky said. "Engine blocks do."

Using the side mirror, Shepherd adjusted it to look over the hood at the attackers.

"Bunch of dudes dressed in hoodies with flak jackets and motor-cycle helmets."

"Rebels," Mako said. "Under Tiberius."

"That neanderthal on the wanted poster," Red said.

"He controls much of this area," Mako said. "I don't know why he's attacking the border guards, but it is of concern."

"Welcome to Russia," Red said.

"If it has anything to do with our arrival, it could be a major prob-lem," Mako said.

"Easy protection job." Lucky raised an eyebrow.

Shepherd shot a look over Mako's head at Lucky.

"Bolivia?" he asked.

"I don't think we have a choice," she said.

Red nodded. "I know this one."

Lucky laughed. "Of course you do."

"Why are you laughing? This is not funny," Mako said.

"You're right," Shepherd said solemnly. "Gallows humor. To relieve stress when we're totally screwed."

"What?" Mako said. "Uncle Max usually doesn't make mistakes like this."

"What mistake?" Red asked.

"Sending protection that tells me we're screwed."

"Don't worry." Lucky peeked her head above the hood before quickly ducking back down when a flurry of gunfire peppered it. "We got this."

Her words were drowned out by the thunderous boom of a massive explosion.

8

Pete Brody cast a nervous glance at the armed guards who stood silently watching as he unloaded his suitcases from the van in front of the high-rise building he'd been told housed the employees.

They'd given him an envelope containing four keycards they said would give him and his family access to the residential building and allow him to access his office in the building across the street.

His family huddled in the doorway of the building where he'd told them to wait.

The rain had stopped but the ground was muddy. Each time he set a suitcase down, dirty drops of mud splattered.

But he was in too big a hurry to worry about it. The guards had told the bus driver he had five minutes to unload and leave the compound. The bus driver was helping Pete.

Suddenly Liz was at his side. "Here, let me wheel these two over."

He gave her a relieved grin as she grabbed the handle on two of the suitcases.

She didn't return the smile, only shook her head.

In the doorway, Cassidy and Will were squabbling and complaining.

"I hate it here," he heard Cassidy say.

"This was the worst idea Dad has ever had," Will said.

Pete's heart sank when he didn't hear Liz defend him.

Instead, she said nothing.

"I don't want him over there with that guy with guns," Cassidy said. "What if they shoot him?"

"They're here to protect him, not hurt him," he heard Liz say. "They're on our side."

As she said the words, Pete looked up and met her eyes.

Just then the suitcase he'd unloaded burst open and clothes fell everywhere onto the muddy ground.

Will laughed. Cassidy screamed. "That's not funny. Those are my clothes. Now they're all wet and muddy."

"Stay here," Liz said, and once again rushed over to help her husband.

"One minute," the guard said.

Crouched down in the mud, Liz and Pete frantically shoved their belongings into the suitcase.

"I'll get this," Liz said. "Grab the last bag."

The bus drove away as Pete and Liz struggled to pull the suitcases across the muddy ground toward the doorway.

Pete was pulling one bag with a broken wheel and trying to keep the other broken suitcase from spilling open again by clutching the sides together.

Finally, all the suitcases and the entire family stood in the alcove. Will reached down and unzipped a suitcase, rummaging around before withdrawing a stuffed kangaroo.

"You're such a baby," Cassidy said. "I gave up stuffed animals when I was eight."

"I did, too," Will said. "Joey's different."

"I kept my stuffed pony when I went to college." Liz ruffled Will's hair. "And your dad bought me a teddy bear when we were dating. You're never too old for a lovie."

Up close, Pete saw that while the building's alcove was dry, it was filthy. The walls were covered in mold. The glass door was smeared with years of fingerprints. A glimpse of the small lobby showed tile floors black with grime. A small wood table with what looked like mail on top was missing a leg and lopsided.

"You sure this is the right place?" Water dripped down Liz's face from her wet hair.

"That building looks nicer." Will gestured at the high-rise across the street.

"Yup, sport," Pete said, and began to turn toward the front door to open it. "This is it. That's what the guard told us."

"Why don't we get to stay in that one?" Cassidy asked.

"Yes, why don't we?" Liz echoed.

"Hey!" Pete said suddenly. "That must be Mr. Cryer."

They all turned to look at a black SUV with tinted windows pulling into the compound.

The vehicle headed straight to the building across the road and parked.

"It's him!" Pete said. "Come on, let's go meet him. Quick!"

"Shouldn't we wait for dinner?" Liz said, but Pete had already grabbed Will's hand and was halfway across the street.

"I just want to give him a quick thank you," Pete said over his shoulder.

"Come on," she said to Cassidy, who made a face.

Liz could see from the look on Cryer's face that the move was a mistake.

The older man had gotten out of the SUV with a scowl and looked around nervously, his head swiveling.

He nearly jumped when Pete appeared before him holding Will's hand.

"Mr. Cryer!" he said in a loud voice. "I just wanted to take a minute to introduce myself and my family and thank you—"

"And you are?" Cryer said, looking past Pete at Lockwood, who was just getting out of the SUV.

"Sorry, sir. I'm Pete Brody, your new engineer."

Cryer didn't respond.

By then Liz and Will had also crossed the street, but they stood back.

Pete continued.

"We can discuss it more at dinner but I'm really excited to talk to you about my plans to make your factory a zero emissions plant. I was looking at the blueprints and we can use one of the runoff tunnels and convert it to clean water for the nearby village and make it a truly green company, sir."

Cryer stared at Pete as if he were speaking a foreign language. His eyes looked slightly crazed.

Pete stopped mid-sentence and glanced at Liz.

"What I think my husband is trying to say—Hi, I'm Elizabeth Brody, by the way."

Just then two burly men with long hair and goatees moved in, enveloping Cryer in their fold and moving him toward the door.

Pete looked on, his brow furrowed in confusion.

A man with a beard and tortoise-shell glasses stepped in front of the Brody family.

"I'm Michael Lockwood. Mr. Cryer has a lot on his plate right now," he said smoothly. "I'm sure he'll be happy to discuss all your ideas once those matters are settled."

9

Shepherd peeked over the hood in time to see a rebel fighter in a green hoodie yank a rocket launcher out of a pickup truck and prop it on the tailgate pointing toward them.

"Incoming! We got to move now! Now!"

Shepherd darted out from behind the SUV and led the others toward a guard shack near the pedestrian border crossing. A few seconds before they reached the shack, the SUV went up in flames behind them and rocked over onto its side.

A burst of gunfire followed the blast.

Lucky had pushed Mako during the sprint, with Red bringing up the rear. When the scatter of gunfire spread toward them, Lucky grabbed Mako and dove for cover behind the guard shack, landing heavily.

"Damn it."

It was Red.

He hadn't made it. He'd had to return and duck behind the overturned, charred SUV. As they watched, he army-crawled toward a border guard's body, snatched the man's gun from his dead hands, and was back behind the smoking SUV before anyone was any wiser.

"Nice move, old man," Shepherd said across the expanse.

Red winked in acknowledgement.

The trio stood and brushed themselves off.

"Are you hurt?" Shepherd leaned down to check on Mako.

"She's fine," Lucky said sharply.

Shepherd raised an eyebrow, but Lucky ignored him and peeked around the shed. She ducked back in time to avoid a bullet that ricocheted off the corner of the metal-sided building.

"The gate to the pedestrian tunnel is open," she said to the others. "It's about ten feet to our left."

"Are we sitting ducks once we're inside?" Shepherd asked.

"No. It quickly winds behind this building. We'd be across the border in seconds."

"Let's do it."

Lucky met Red's eyes. "Unless you need us, we're going in," she said.

"I got this," he shouted. "On the count of five."

"Come on," Lucky shouted, and pushed Mako in front of her. "You're going to run faster than you ever have in your life."

"What about Red?" Mako frowned.

Lucky just shook her head.

"We can't—" Mako said.

Her words were interrupted by a bloodcurdling scream as Red began to shout and fire the submachine gun from his hiding spot.

"Move! Move! Move!" Lucky shouted, pushing Mako forward as she ran alongside, shielding her with her body. Shepherd was behind them, nearly pressed up against them as he ran.

They slipped through the gate just in time to see Red sprint from his hiding place and take shelter behind the guard shack in the cover they'd just vacated.

Shepherd paused. "I can't leave the old man here."

"I agree," Mako said.

"He'll be fine." Lucky pulled on Shepherd's sleeve. "He's going to be here to meet us when we're done, just like he said. Guy is solid as they come."

Shepherd grumbled, "He should've never come with us in the first place."

"You're right," Lucky said. "Now let's go."

Right when they emerged through the chain link cage surrounding the pedestrian crossing, a guard charged Lucky with his gun raised, shouting something in Russian.

Without pausing, Shepherd reached over and plucked the gun from the man's hands and shot an elbow up to the man's chin. The man fell to the ground, out cold.

"That's one for me," Shepherd said.

All the other guards were up on the skyway firing at the attacking rebels.

Lucky reached down and searched the man's pockets. She stood triumphantly holding a set of car keys. The trio raced to an adjacent parking lot, keeping low behind the cars as Lucky pressed the alarm until she found the vehicle.

It was a brown Humvee.

"Let's go!" Shepherd shouted.

They piled in the vehicle and peeled out in a cloud of dust, heading toward the Russian heartland.

10

Paxton Cryer paced in front of the floor-to-ceiling windows of his suite on the penthouse level of the tower. The windows were on two sides— the sides that faced away from the plastics factory and the decrepit high-rise next door that housed the workers.

He knew that the other building where his employees lived was nearly empty on this day.

The workers, most of them Muslim, had cleared out to visit family to celebrate Mawlid, the Islamic holiday celebrating the prophet Muhammad's birthday. Giving the workers a few days off to celebrate hadn't been Cryer's idea. Lockwood had told him if he didn't approve the time off, the rest of the world would hear about it and Cryer Plastics would look bad.

Cryer had argued only briefly before conceding. The last thing he needed was for his company to look bad. At least until he could sell it and become an oligarch.

He surveyed the Russian landscape that spread out before him from his sky-high perch.

A light snow had begun to fall since his arrival, and the desolate wasteland far below actually looked slightly pleasant for once. He'd never liked this view but also felt that it was somewhat comforting to stand so high above everyone else and see for miles around. Nobody would show up at his fortified compound without him knowing about it.

He also liked that the closest village was more than a mile away.

That meant fewer prying eyes. It was nobody's business what he was doing with his factory. Or rather, what he wasn't doing. The sooner he sold off the company to Tiberius, the better. He just needed to have Lockwood think he was actually the one brokering the hostage deal. He trusted Lockwood to a certain extent, but not when it came to a secret twenty-million-dollar deal with a rebel warlord.

Behind him, he heard Lockwood refill their drinks from the mirrored bar that took up a corner of the suite. The clink of ice in the crystal soothed Cryer. It made this shithole seem less isolated. The wafting notes of Beethoven's Sonata No. 14 in C-Sharp Minor coming out of his surround-sound speaker system also helped class up the joint.

His black and gray suite was done up in fine leather and chrome. He knew his workers' eyeballs would pop out if they ever saw how opulent it was.

He looked over at the original Matisse on the wall. It was small but served its purpose as a decoy. Any thief would go for that painting and leave the black-and-white picture of him as a ten-year-old on his parents' farm safely on the wall.

In the photograph he was riding on the back of one of the big mares. A sweet, brown-eyed girl named Maddie. His father was walking along beside him holding the reins. He was smiling at the camera but Cryer never forgot the words he'd said immediately after the shutter clicked. "You'll never be able to fill my shoes, son. You just aren't that smart. Unfortunately, you took after your mother in that department, God rest her soul. But you're really good with the animals. You got that from her. So don't worry. I've got a place for you. Your brother John will run the company and you can live here and run the farm. I think you'll make a fine ranch hand."

It was appropriate that this photo be hung in front of the safe that contained most of Cryer's fortune—millions in cash and a priceless diamond.

After leaking news of the kidnapping to the international media, he knew he'd be able to justify borrowing twenty million dollars from the company to save the man's life. Nobody needed to know that half of that ransom would line his own pockets.

That, along with the millions in his vault and the diamond, would set him up for life. He would be just like the Russian oligarchs he summered with in the South of France. He would finally be on their level. The diamond was his ticket.

He'd anonymously bought "The Key 2317," a coveted 101-carat pear-shaped diamond, by converting part of his vast fortune into cryptocurrency. When the rare diamond came up for auction at Sotheby's last year, he'd bought it and then immediately flew to Russia to stash it in his fortified compound. It was his retirement fund and safety net. Nobody would ever look for it here.

And nobody would ever think the goofy picture of him on a horse would hide the access panel to a vault containing all his treasures.

That day on the horse had been a defining moment in Cryer's life. Too bad his father hadn't lived long enough to be proven wrong. But then again, neither had his brother John.

For a while, their deaths when the company's Cessna crashed had seemed like the worst day in Cryer's life. Until he realized it was actually the best one.

Lockwood handed Cryer his drink.

Cryer took a sip. "This vodka is much better than the Russian swill you can buy around here."

"If you say so."

Immediately Cryer shot Lockwood a look, but the other man was shuffling through some papers.

Cryer turned back to the window.

Out of the gray, a pair of headlights emerged in the distance.

"Who is that?"

Lockwood looked up.

"I expect that is Courtney Mako."

"The timing on this is terrible."

"Just point her toward the files. That's due diligence. She can slog through it on her own. You should stay and chat for a bit and then excuse yourself, saying you need to meet with a new employee who just arrived from America."

"That's right. What's the fellow's name again?"

"Brody. Pete Brody."

"That's right, Brady."

"Brody."

"You take those twins with you but don't be gone long. I don't like being unprotected here," Cryer said.

"I'll make it a quick meet," Lockwood said. "We'll see what his demands are and then we will arrange to do the exchange in the morning. By tomorrow night we should be on a plane back home."

"Perfect," Cryer said.

"I'm going to brief the brothers now, if you don't mind."

"No, no, go ahead." Cryer waved his hand. "Bring them in."

Lockwood opened the thick wooden doors to the suite. The Darcy brothers were stationed on each side of the door. Each one was heavily armed.

He gestured for them to come inside.

They wore shoulder holsters over pressed black shirts and semi-automatic rifles on straps across their chests.

"We leave to meet the rebel leader in ten minutes," Lockwood began. "He's dangerous, but he's not going to do anything during this meeting. He knows that if he does, there will be no exchange. He wants money and probably a lot of it. We're safe until he gets it."

"Understood," one of the brothers said.

Cryer stepped away from the window. "His point is, boys, that you need to keep your mitts off your trigger finger. We need those hostages alive. I need to count on your utmost discretion and self-control. This is a meeting only. This cannot blow up in our face. Have I made myself clear?"

The brothers paused for a second and exchanged a look before broad grins spread simultaneously across their handsome faces and they said unanimously, "Crystal clear, sir."

11

Mako was practically in the front seat with Lucky and Shepherd as she leaned forward, neck craning to see the imposing compound on the horizon.

Huge, slushy snowflakes splashed on the windshield before the wipers sent them flying. The heat was on high and they could still see their breath as they spoke.

"It's about as dismal as I imagined," Lucky said.

"It looks like a fortress. I'd think the location being so isolated alone would make it safe, but those towers are manned with armed guards," Mako said.

Lucky reached down to the floor and lifted the assault weapon they'd taken from the border guard onto her lap. She was examining it when Mako spoke up.

"Before we arrive, I want to make one thing clear. This is an investigation. I'm here to examine Cryer's financials in person. Uncle Max has not declared him an enemy. This is just a way for us to resolve the discrepancy I came across."

"We get that," Shepherd said, meeting her eyes in the rearview mirror.

"Then why is *she* treating it like an assault?" Mako pointed at Lucky holding the weapon.

"When people start going missing, and stuff starts blowing up, it's no longer an investigation. It's survival," Lucky said calmly.

"That was not my understanding. You are here simply to provide security and keep me safe."

"Exactly what we did back there," Lucky said in a matter-of-fact voice.

"You heard Red," Shepherd said. "Our number one priority is keeping you safe, but we're also going to find two employees. From the looks of it, people don't just disappear around here. Where would they go?"

Mako didn't respond, only pursed her lips tighter.

Shepherd met her eyes in the mirror but quickly looked away.

"Well, when we get there, I'm in charge," Mako said. "I'm the one who will be giving orders. You are here to accompany and assist me first. Missing employees second. For all we know they went out on a bender somewhere or went AWOL because this place is a nightmare."

"You're the boss," Shepherd said.

Lucky glared at him.

He widened his eyes and quickly said, "Lucky here takes her job very seriously, that's all. We both do. Our job is to keep you alive and sometimes that involves, um, some—"

"Violence," Lucky cut him off. "You can call it an assault, but we call it defensive measures. If someone is shooting a gun at you, what do you want us to do?"

"I want you to guard me and get me to safety."

"Right," Shepherd said. "No argument there."

This time Lucky rolled her eyes at him.

"And sometimes it involves killing people," she said. "It sounds like you were led to believe otherwise."

"All I'm saying," Mako said, matching Lucky's calm and reasonable tone, "is that your gun won't be necessary once we're inside the compound. Do you agree?"

"No." Lucky gave a scoffing laugh. "We're just going to have to agree to disagree on that one."

"Look, they're opening the gate for us," Shepherd said.

Both women ignored him.

Mako sat back in her seat and folded her arms across her chest.

When the guards came up to the driver's side window, Mako leaned forward.

"I'm Courtney Mako and these two people are my security."

"We've been expecting you," the guard said, and waved them through.

Mako turned to Lucky with a smug smile. "See? Brains over brawn works best."

Lucky stared at the other woman for a long moment and then turned toward the window, her expression unreadable.

They were directed to the tower on the right, which had an ornate front entrance with a chandelier and two sets of doors.

"Wait here. Mark Wilson will be down to escort you in a few minutes."

Ten minutes later, a thin, tall man in a rumpled suit appeared.

After introductions, Wilson led them to the elevator.

"I assume you will want to get started right away?" he asked, then, without waiting for an answer, continued. "Cryer is waiting for you in his suite and he'll escort you to his office to examine the files."

"I thought Michael Lockwood was going to be showing me around?" Mako asked with a tight smile as they stepped into the elevator.

Wilson's face grew slightly paler. "He's not here."

"I thought they flew in together from London?"

"Yeah," Wilson said, and then became very busy with his phone.

"You seem a little uncomfortable with me asking about Lockwood," Mako said. "Is he okay?"

Wilson shrugged. "Things have been a little strange around here, but from what I know he's just fine."

"Strange as in missing employees?" Mako said.

"Tell us where Lockwood is," Shepherd said.

Wilson held up his phone.

"He's in the middle of nowhere. Well, the middle of nowhere about twenty minutes from here. Some meeting that apparently I'm not important enough to go to even though I'm supposed to be Cryer's executive assistant."

Shepherd raised an eyebrow at Lucky.

"You're tracking Lockwood?" he asked.

"It's just a find-your-phone type deal. We've had two men disappear in the past few days. Cryer wants me to keep an eye on Lockwood. He said I was in charge of making sure nothing happened to him. Like, how am I supposed to do that? I'm an executive, not a thug." He winced. "No offense."

"When did this Lockwood guy leave?" Shepherd asked.

"Ten minutes ago, right before I got the call you were here," he said. "I don't know what the meeting is about but I'm assuming it has to do with our missing men. All I have is this showing me where he is. It's not like I can teleport to go save him if he is in danger. And what did Cryer mean I need to make sure nothing happens to Lockwood? I think I should start getting hazard pay. Two of the managers just up and disappeared? What if I'm next? This was supposed to be a secure compound. I mean look around. Are they going to come in here and get me next?"

Wilson's voice was growing frantic.

"Nobody's coming in anywhere," Mako said.

Shepherd shot Lucky a look. She rolled her eyes.

"I'm supposedly Mr. Cryer's executive assistant here," Wilson said. "But as soon as he arrives, it's like I'm persona non grata."

"That sucks." It was the first thing Lucky had said since they met.

He glanced over at her, and she smiled. "I'm sure you keep this place running smoothly when he's away, and that's nothing to sneeze at."

Mako narrowed her eyes at Lucky.

"If you don't mind, I think we should go check on Mr. Lockwood and make sure he's safe," Shepherd said. "You have enough to deal with now that Cryer is back. Keeping employees safe is not your job. But it is ours."

"Exactly what I was thinking," Lucky added.

"I'm not sure that's okay. It sounded like a secret meeting," he said.

"We'll be discreet," Lucky said. Behind Wilson's back, Mako shook her head.

"We'll just need to borrow that." Lucky plucked the phone out of Wilson's hands. "I'll get it back to you before anyone is wiser."

"It's fine. It's a spare company phone."

"Perfect," she said.

Shepherd punched the elevator at the next floor.

"Wait!" Wilson reached into his pocket and handed out three keycards. "These should give you all the access you need."

Without answering, Shepherd and Lucky stepped out of the open elevator door.

"Where are you going?" Mako sounded panicked.

"Stairs," he said. "You go on up and deal with Cryer. We'll catch up to you later."

The elevator door closed on Mako, her mouth wide open.

12

The wind howled, sending its creeping icy fingers through every small crack in the hunting shed.

When they'd arrived at the shed, Lockwood had been sure the Darcy brothers had not properly followed the GPS coordinates he'd given them.

But then he saw a crude painting of a wolf's head on the side of the shed and knew this was where he would be meeting the warlord, who had appeared on international television wearing a wolf skin over his combat clothing.

Now, inside, Lockwood tugged on his fur-lined cap and wished his North Face jacket was longer and warmer.

He watched as the Darcy brothers paced the small room like panthers. They didn't say much, just strode back and forth across the wooden floor as if they had energy to burn.

Lockwood tried to stay out of their way. He stood in a corner, warily eyeing what looked like a large puddle of dried blood staining the middle of the floor. The Darcy brothers trod over the stain as if it didn't even exist. He had made a wide circle around it, feeling superstitious, as if he were avoiding walking over someone's grave.

Every once in a while, an uncontrollable shiver ran the length of his body.

It wasn't just the bitter cold of the unheated room that sent icy chills down his spine. A dark sense of foreboding had overcome him the instant they walked into the unlocked hunting shack. It had taken a few seconds for one of the brothers to find a light switch, and while he stood in the dark, Lockwood could have sworn he felt another presence in the space—so much so that he was actually surprised when the over-head lights flickered on to reveal an empty room.

There was also a biting smell that made his eyes water.

A few seconds later he realized what it was—bleach.

It was a very unsettling detail to notice.

"I thought your guy was supposed to be here already?" Connor Darcy said.

Lockwood realized he was sweating even though the room was ice cold.

"I don't know. I'm just doing as I was told."

The other brother, Clint, frowned.

"I don't like this."

"Don't you guys have guns?" Lockwood said.

The brothers patted their sides.

"We got enough for right now," Clint said. "We don't want to cause an international incident."

"We got the big boys in the SUV," Connor added.

"Okay," Lockwood said nervously.

A low rumbling and vibration filled the room.

"That might be him. Let me check."

Connor Darcy opened the door and stepped outside.

He left the door open and yelled back, "Headlights coming. Vehicles on approach. We're a go."

Clint said, "Come on. We're not going to wait for them here like sitting ducks. We'll meet them out in the open air."

The two stepped outside into the brisk night air, their breath visible under the large spotlight above the front door. In the distance, two small lights bounced on the horizon.

One of the brothers stooped down. When he straightened, he was holding a small, shiny white square.

"Is this one of your missing guys?" He handed Lockwood the square. An employee ID with the name Drake Martin.

Lockwood closed his eyes for a second and felt bile rise in his mouth.

"This is not good," he said. "This is not good."

"Don't worry. We're experts at this sort of stuff," Connor said.

As the three waited, more lights appeared.

"We've got a regular convoy coming," Clint said.

Lockwood swore softly.

"It's all good, man," Connor said.

"We've been outnumbered way worse than this before, right, brother?"

"Right. That one time we had, what, two dozen guys attacking us?"

"Reckon it was about that many."

"This isn't a battle," Lockwood said in a high-pitched whine. "We're just meeting."

"Sure. We know. Good idea to always be prepared for things to head south."

"Sort of our motto," Connor said.

The three stood silently for a few seconds watching the oncoming convoy.

The first vehicle, a black SUV, arrived and stopped about twenty yards from the shack. Three similar black SUVs parked in a row beside the first, all facing the shack. Their headlights shone on the trio.

The Darcy brothers didn't move.

Lockwood flinched. "We're just sitting ducks here."

"Not really, pal," Clint said. "Unless they want to shoot right through the front windshield, they're gonna have to roll down a window or open a door first."

"That gives us all the time we need," his brother said.

"If you say so." Lockwood's voice shook.

Then, as if someone pushed a button, the headlights on all but the first SUV went out.

Two men opened the doors of that vehicle.

The Darcy brothers tensed and reached inside their coats, keeping their hands on their weapons as the men stepped out. They wore full military gear with flak jackets and helmets.

They stood beside the hood, assault rifles slung over their shoulders and resting on their chests.

Then the back door opened and a man emerged.

As he stood to his full height, Lockwood made a small sound.

It was Tiberius.

He wore a camouflage parka with a wolf skin over it. His fatigue pants were tucked into black combat boots with thick soles and treads. He had a thick beard and mustache below a bulbous, pockmarked nose.

But it wasn't his imposing figure that had Lockwood starting to hyperventilate. It was the two giant wolves that crawled out of the backseat and were now standing on each side of the man.

Lockwood was staring. Clint Darcy nudged him.

Lockwood looked up, flustered. "I'm Michael Lockwood. I'll be standing in for Mr. Cryer."

Tiberius frowned.

"Mr. Cryer was supposed to be here."

"I'm here to receive your request and bring it back to Mr. Cryer."

Tiberius closed his eyes for a second and shook his head.

When he opened his eyes again, he squinted at Lockwood.

"Tell Mr. Cryer that I will release his man in exchange for twenty million dollars and the diamond he has squirreled away at the compound."

The Darcy brothers exchanged a quick look.

"You said 'man.' There are two men missing." Lockwood swallowed hard.

"Not anymore."

Lockwood's face seemed to go through a range of emotions. First, all the color drained from his cheeks, and then they turned bright red. He swallowed and tried to speak but nothing came out.

Finally, he managed, "Mr. Cryer can't get that kind of money together. Not in cash, at least."

Tiberius leaned back and roared in laughter. "Oh, yes, he can. If you don't know this, he sent the wrong man to speak with me."

Then Tiberius narrowed his eyes. "Or maybe you do know this and are trying to bluff me. In that case, again, you were the wrong man to send on this job."

Backing up, Lockwood held out his palms. "I know he has a lot of cash. I know he has the diamond. But I don't know how much money he has. I'm not privy to that information."

"And yet the operations manager was aware of this?" Tiberius asked. He nodded, and one of the SUV's doors swung open.

Drake Martin was pushed outside. A man in fatigues stood behind him, holding him by the collar with one hand. The other hand had a gun stuck into Drake's back between the shoulder blades. Two other men stood at his side, holding him by the arms. His mouth was gagged and his hands bound behind his back. A chain tied his ankles together.

"Here is my request, as you so eloquently put it," Tiberius said. "I request that Mr. Cryer bring me the twenty million and the diamond and I'll allow this man to live."

He paused for a long second.

Lockwood waited.

"If Mr. Cryer doesn't agree to my terms, this man will be the second Cryer Plastics employee I kill. And then I will kill every person who works for Mr. Cryer until I get to him. And then I'll kill him."

"If he has the money, I will attempt to convince him..."

Drake's eyes grew wide. He shook his head.

"Wrong answer," Tiberius said. "I'm done playing games. This is not a negotiation. I'll come get the money and diamond without your help."

He reached for a whistle from a long cord around his neck and lifted it to his lips.

Then he made a clicking sound. The wolves snarled and raced toward Drake, who began to thrash and struggle. The two men holding his arms tightened their grip.

The growling wolves stopped in front of Drake with their hair on end and their lips snarled.

"Being torn to shreds by hungry wolves is the most painful way to die," he said. "Basically you are eaten alive. Ask your man here. He witnessed his colleague die this way. It's not pretty."

"Stop! Stop! I'll get you the money and the diamond!" Lockwood shouted.

Drake began to thrash against the two men holding him. One punched him in the jaw and Drake stopped struggling. He hung his head.

"I'll get it!" Lockwood shouted. "I'll make sure to get it!"

Tiberius made another clicking sound and the wolves turned and loped back to his side.

"I need it in a few hours."

"Fine," Lockwood said in a frantic voice. "I'll have it."

"And tell Cryer not to forget the diamond," Tiberius said.

Tiberius was about to turn around to get back in his vehicle when he froze. Everyone heard the sound at once—a vehicle approaching fast.

But there were no headlights.

All heads turned to search the darkness.

Then a vehicle popped over a small hill, and a Humvee came barreling through the night.

The Darcy brothers shoved Lockwood into the shack and drew their weapons. The Humvee came to a skidding stop just as Tiberius's men jumped out of their vehicles and let loose a volley of gunfire toward both the Darcy brothers and the Humvee.

The move triggered a chaotic gunfight with three different groups firing upon one another. The Darcy brothers took cover behind their own SUV, which was parked close to the shack.

"Cover me while I grab the hostage," Clint said to his brother.

Connor stepped out from the cover of the SUV and laid down a barrage of bullets as Clint raced toward Drake.

But before he could reach him, Drake reeled back with a howl and collapsed on the ground near one of the vehicles.

At the same time, Connor's cover attempt drew a flurry of fire from several rebels who all turned their weapons toward him. He dove behind one of the vehicles, but not before a bullet found him. After he rolled to one side, he sat up and surveyed the damage on his leg. It looked like a through-and-through shot to the lower leg. The blood was minimal. He wouldn't be able to run fast, but he could still shoot. He stood up in time to see three men descending on him with their weapons drawn.

13

As the Humvee crested a small hill, Lucky saw the line of SUVs parked in front of the small shack. She scanned the scene quickly through her binoculars.

"We found them. But it looks like they've got a lot of company."

"Keep talking," Shepherd said. "We're coming in hot. I need the situation."

He was in the driver's seat, leaning forward, white-knuckling the steering wheel.

"Four, no, five vehicles. Everyone looks armed. Rebels."

"Do you see Cryer's men? And the suit—Lockwood?" Shepherd said quickly.

"I see a suit. He's got two bodyguards flanking him. And there is somebody tied up facing them. Guarded by the rebels."

"The missing employee?"

"Roger that," she said. "Brace yourself! Incoming!"

As soon as the words left her mouth, gunfire hit the Humvee.

Shepherd skidded to a stop perpendicular to the other vehicles.

He and Lucky immediately bailed out the driver's side door and ducked behind the engine block as bullets rained down on the vehicle.

Poking his head up, Shepherd grabbed the assault rifle and took a few well-aimed shots at the closest rebels, managing to hit three of them. Meanwhile, the gun battle was going full tilt between the two sides in front of them.

"I need a weapon." Lucky scowled.

"I'll get you one. Stand by."

She waited by the front of the truck.

Shepherd fired again.

Then, out of the corner of his mouth, he said, "Go around the front. There's a dead rebel with a weapon at your ten o'clock. I'll lay down some suppressive fire to give you a chance to grab it."

While Shepherd held the gunmen at bay, Lucky raced around the Humvee, grabbed the weapon, and then dove behind the engine block.

Seconds after she returned, Shepherd heard a sound. He turned in time to see that one of the rebels had made a wide circle and was creeping around to the back of the Humvee. He had a machete and was just about to bring it down on the back of Lucky's head when Shepherd put a bullet through his forehead.

Lucky jumped and whirled, seeing the rebel fall dead to the ground behind her. "What the?"

"That's one for me," he said.

Lucky took a position behind the hood of the Humvee, resting her rifle on the hood and scanning for danger. Then she spotted the rebel leader.

He was staring right at her.

Fighters surrounded him. He made a loud clicking noise and two huge wolves loped over and stood at his side. He made another noise and they followed him as he slid into a nearby SUV, never taking his eyes off Lucky.

At the same time, two rebels hefted Drake up from the ground where he lay bleeding and shoved him into another vehicle.

Shepherd was about to charge the SUV when Lucky tackled him to the ground.

Right after they hit the dirt, a man hanging out one of the SUV's windows ripped off a few rounds from a .50-caliber M2 Browning machine gun that peppered the snowy ground around them.

After a few seconds, Lucky and Shepherd sat up and watched as the two vehicles disappeared into the night.

Shepherd stood and held out his hand to help Lucky up. She stood, brushed herself off, and said, "That's one for me."

He frowned.

14

It was a standoff.

The two Darcy brothers faced Lucky and Shepherd. All four had their guns pointed. All four were shivering.

"Lower your weapons," Connor Darcy shouted.

"You first," Lucky responded.

Shepherd gave a low chuckle.

So did Clint Darcy.

"You guys sure know how to show up and ruin a party," Clint said.

"We're used to being the party," Lucky smirked. "That's how it works around here."

"Around here? You're as American as us," Connor said.

"Wrong," Lucky answered. "He is. I'm not."

"You a Russian?" Connor said.

"Can we talk about this inside?" Lockwood huffed. "I'm freezing."

"Who are you, anyway? Why are you here in the middle of nowhere Russia right when we're about to do a deal?" Connor asked.

"Uncle Max sent us," Shepherd said.

"Uncle who?"

Lockwood exhaled loudly and put his arm in front of Clint Darcy, who had raised his gun toward Shepherd when he spoke.

"They're legit," he said. "They're watchdogs for one of the main shareholders."

"Aha," Connor said. "Here to start trouble?"

"We're here to keep idiots alive." Lucky put her hands on her hips. "And get back some hostages."

"There's only one left," Clint said. "And that's our job."

"One left? And you've been here for how long? Guess we got here just in time," Lucky said archly.

"Guy was dead before we were in country. Now, thanks to you, we might lose the other one. You guys were the ones who created this SNAFU. Not us," Connor said.

"Hey." Shepherd put his palms in the air. "We thought you were under attack."

"We were negotiating." Clint glared at him.

"We were just evening the playing field," Shepherd said. "Looked like you were outnumbered."

"Can we please go inside now?" Lockwood asked.

"It was under control," Clint said.

"Really?" Lucky asked.

"It was under control until you guys showed up and started a war with a rebel leader."

Shepherd and Lucky exchanged a look.

Lucky swore softly under her breath.

"What's up with the wolf man?" she asked. "What do the wolves do?"

"They're weapons," Clint said.

"Our intelligence is that when he blows a whistle, they attack to kill," Lockwood said. "We need to get back immediately. This is really, really bad. I had this under control."

He gestured to the bodies the rebel leader had left sprawled in the snow-covered clearing. "Cryer is going to kill me. Do you realize what you've done?"

"Apparently we saved your life only to have Cryer take it?" Lucky shrugged.

Clint Darcy burst out laughing.

Lucky gave him a slight smile.

Shepherd looked from one to the other and frowned.

"Are we going to sit here all day and chitchat?" he said.

"Forget talking in the shack. You guys have talked way too much. Now that we've worked that out, can we agree that we all need to get back to the factory immediately?" Lockwood said. "They're going to regroup and come after us."

"You're sure of this?" Lucky asked.

"That hostage you were trying to save? He told the rebels about a safe Cryer has at the compound with millions of dollars in cash and a priceless diamond."

Connor Darcy gave a low whistle. "Would've been nice to know about all this before we got here, Lockwood."

Walking away, Clint laughed. "They talked about it in the car ride here. Sort of," he said. "It wasn't obvious to a knucklehead like you, but if you were paying attention you would've figured it out. Our boy Cryer is sitting on a golden egg and Wolf Man aims to get it."

"You didn't seem afraid of him." Clint looked at Lucky with admiration.

"I've dealt with worse."

His grin grew wider.

Shepherd cleared his throat loudly.

"Let's gather up all these weapons and fortify the castle," he said.

The four of them plucked all the guns from the bodies and then headed back to their vehicles. As they walked, Shepherd lifted his forearm and said in a low voice,

"Red? You out there?"

Nothing. He frowned. "Something's wrong with my wrist comm."

"I know when I hit that one rebel, he turned and struck my wrist and arm," Lucky said. "It still stings. Let me try."

"Red?"

At least Lucky's wrist comm responded with some static noise. But no voice.

"Uncle Max?" she tried.

"Anyone?"

After hopping inside their vehicle, Lucky grabbed her phone from a small backpack she was wearing. Then she swore softly. "It's dead. Try yours."

Keeping one hand on the wheel, Shepherd pulled out his phone and handed it to her. She tried to make a call. "Nope," she said, and tossed it into his lap. "Just like Red said. Let's try our wrist comms again."

She lifted her forearm. "Red? Can you read me?"

Holding up his arm, Shepherd spoke as well.

"Red?"

No answer.

Shepherd turned on the interior light and looked down at his wrist.

His eyes grew wide and he held up his forearm. "Look. What do you think that's from?"

Lucky squinted. "If I didn't know better I'd say it deflected a bullet."

"No way."

There was some slight static from Lucky's wrist.

They both widened their eyes.

"Fox? Can you read me?"

It was Red using Lucky's nickname. He sounded far away, his voice nearly obscured by static.

Not sure how long the connection would last, Lucky didn't spare any words.

"We need extraction, Red. The shit has hit the fan. Do you read? Extraction needed asap."

They waited for a response.

Lucky shook her wrist. She put her head down to it, listening.

Nothing.

Not even static.

Shepherd shook his head and started the engine.

"Hope he got the message."

15

Right outside Paxton Cryer's large personal suite were two smaller offices with glass walls. Both were filled with bookshelves, filing cabinets, and a large boardroom-type table.

Courtney Mako was in one office, sitting at the table with a slew of files spread out in an orderly fashion before her.

She was leaning over a stack of papers wearing oversized reading glasses. Her heels were on the floor and her feet curled up on the chair under her. Her hair was pulled back in a messy bun held in place by a pencil.

Her lips were moving.

To an outsider, it appeared Mako was speaking to herself.

But a small voice was coming from her wrist comm.

Uncle Max.

"What about that monthly payment?" he asked.

"I just can't reconcile it," she said. "It makes no sense. I don't see any other glaring discrepancies. But this monthly cash withdrawal is a definite red flag."

"The guy's got an entire team of ex-wives," Max said. "Maybe he's paying off one of them under the table. Maybe she knows things she shouldn't."

"Your vivid imagination is why you are a billionaire, but I think you're giving both Cryer and the ex-wife too much credit," she said.

"A girlfriend? Mistress?"

"Hmmm," Mako said. "That would make more sense. He's keeping a mistress somewhere…"

"So he's not a crook, just a creep?"

"Well, he is technically separated from his fourth wife."

"You can't possibly be defending him?"

Mako laughed. A rare sound that few people heard.

"Wait." She frowned. "The payments began two years ago and have slowly increased over time."

"Interesting."

"Very."

"Well, keep digging. Make copies. We can always go over it again when you get back."

"I won't need to look at it twice." She shook her head. "You know me, Max. I have a photographic memory."

"No offense intended, but take those pictures anyway so we have documentation."

"Of course," she said. "I'm already doing so."

"Of course you are."

Mako's eyebrows drew together.

"There's another strange thing."

Max waited to speak, not wanting to interrupt her train of thought.

She shuffled some papers and then nodded.

"Yeah. So the way this place is supposed to work is that everybody sends their plastics here to be recycled, right?"

"That's usually how it works."

"So I see that supply chain. But if you recycle the plastic you receive, don't you usually sell it as a recycled product to someone else?"

"Yes."

"What I don't understand is where that profit is. I see nothing in the books that shows the company receives income from selling its recycled products," Mako said. "I don't understand how they are profitable. How are they paying for the plastics that come into their plant to be recycled in the first place?"

"Oh boy," Max said.

"What?"

"People pay a lot of money for someone to take their plastic trash," Max said. "We're talking multi-million dollars. You'd be surprised. In addition, there are a few programs—government-funded programs—that donate plastics from cities, counties, etcetera to these plants. I'd bet the farm that this is Cryer's game—take all the money and do nothing with the plastics."

"Don't even joke about betting it all," Mako said. "I like my job too much, but I think you might be onto something. Let me keep digging. I'll try to find records of the origin of the plastics that end up here."

"If anyone can figure it out, it's you, Mako. I'll let you get back to it. Call me when you know more."

And with that, he was gone.

Mako stared at the bank of filing cabinets in front of her.

She drew back her shoulders and headed toward them.

Her hand was on the handle of a drawer when Shepherd and Lucky burst into the room.

Taking her time, she turned to face them. She raised an eyebrow. "Yes?"

When she saw them, she frowned.

Lucky's hair was disheveled and she had what looked like a smear of blood on her cheek. Shepherd's arm was covered in what looked like motor oil and his hands were caked with dried blood.

"What on earth happened to you?"

"Long story," Shepherd said. "But we might have started a war with a rebel leader."

"You're joking," Mako said in alarm. Her eyes grew wide.

"It wasn't actually our fault." Lucky smiled.

"It's time to go," Shepherd said. "Pack up your stuff. We're leaving immediately."

Mako opened her mouth but no sound came out.

She sputtered for a few seconds and then said, "I'm not going anywhere."

"You're leaving all right." Lucky headed for the table with all the documents spread over it. "Don't bother cleaning this up. We don't have time."

"I just got off the phone with Uncle Max," she said. "He wanted me to look into something new that will take a while."

"You can either come with us and live or you can stay and die," Lucky said. "Your choice."

Shepherd shook his head. "It's not actually that bleak."

Lucky glared at him. "Feel free to stay with her. Your funeral."

Clearing his throat, Shepherd said, "How much time do you need?"

"I'm not sure," Mako replied. "Most likely not too long. I've done the majority of the examination."

"You have until we round up the factory's employees," Lucky said, and stormed out.

16

The wolf handler easily blended into the background at the warehouse, which was just how he liked it. The large space was frenetic with energy as the rebel fighters prepared for battle.

The wolf handler was a nondescript man, and that suited him in many ways. He was small in stature and a man of few words. His ability to become part of the scenery was a tactical advantage he was always keenly aware of. He knew his greatest strength was that people underestimated him. His greatest secret was that despite Tiberius learning how to control the wolves, the wolf handler remained the true alpha. The wolves only listened to Tiberius because the handler had taught them to do so. But the wolves knew who the true alpha was.

Once, when Tiberius had gone off on one of his rants criticizing the wolf handler, he'd put his forearm against the handler's neck. It had taken a quickly spoken code word to stop the wolves from killing the rebel warlord right then.

But Tiberius had been in such a rage he hadn't even noticed.

He hadn't known how close to death he'd been.

Now, the wolf handler watched silently in a corner as Tiberius and his men prepared for battle.

Men in camouflage military gear were checking weapons and vehicles.

This was what they lived for.

They were hired killing machines for a cause.

At least that was how they saw themselves.

But the wolf handler thought they were fools.

They listened blindly to their leader. Their lives hinged on the impetuous and power-hungry man's whims.

Tiberius was unpredictable to a fault. He ruled by fear.

Once, to prove a point, he'd killed his own mistress, ordering the wolves to tear her apart, only to learn that her supposed betrayal had actually been an innocent meeting with a man to arrange a surprise birthday party for Tiberius.

The rebel warlord gave off the appearance of power with his tough words, military gear, wolf skin, and designer accessories, but he rarely stained his own hands with the blood of others. He ordered the wolves to do that for him.

It was distasteful. And cowardly.

The wolf handler always did a good job of hiding his true feelings toward the rebel leader. Even now, as he stood against the wall in a corner of the busy warehouse listening to the tirade spewing from the rebel leader's mouth, his face remained expressionless and his posture relaxed. Inside, though, he felt hatred rise up into his solar plexus.

Tiberius was pacing the warehouse surrounded by two of his top soldiers, raging about the disrespect he'd just been shown by the Cryer Plastics people.

"By this time tomorrow, they'll all be dead," Tiberius said. "I've taken their paltry payments for long enough. They cannot come into my country and tell me what to do. I will take over the company. It will fund my operations as I take over more of this area and this country."

The two men at his side nodded.

The wolf handler narrowed his eyes. Interesting.

"I'd like the new signs to be classier than the ones now. Hire a marketing expert to do the branding. It will say Tiberius Plastics Inc.

Or maybe Tiberius Plastics Co. I haven't decided. But get someone on it. It needs to look modern. And sleek."

"Understood," one of the men said, and scuttled off.

The other man moved close to the warlord's side.

"The storm has arrived. It is nearly whiteout conditions. It will not clear until morning."

"I told you, we need to attack under the cover of darkness."

"It's going to be difficult to navigate," the man said.

Snapping his head to look the man in the eyes, Tiberius's nostrils flared. "I said that we attack under the cover of darkness."

He patted a large metal cylinder the size of a tipped-over filing cabinet that was being placed on the back of a truck with a hoist.

"This is an electromagnetic pulse tactical weapon. Once we shoot it off, anything electronic within a hundred-meter radius will be knocked out. We'll be able to go right through the front gates after it goes off. All of our equipment will be protected in these Faraday bags."

He pointed to a stack of bags that the fighters were grabbing as they passed.

The man swallowed and said meekly, "I will prepare the men."

Then Tiberius turned and looked around until his eyes focused on the wolf handler standing in the shadows.

"Are the dogs ready?"

As he always had to do when it came to the rebel warlord, the handler hid his dismay with his mighty canines being called "dogs."

"The wolves are always ready," he answered simply.

"Very good," Tiberius said.

Then Tiberius looked over at the American hostage who was slumped in a seat near one of the vehicles.

"They look hungry," Tiberius said, peering at the wolves. "Maybe they need a snack before we leave?"

He jutted his chin toward the American, who was covered in dried blood. It looked like it was taking the man a great deal of effort to keep his head up and his eyes open.

"Their appetite is insatiable," the wolf handler said. "It will not affect their desire to hunt."

Realizing that the conversation was about him, the American jerked up his head.

"Wait!" the hostage said in a strangled voice. "You can't kill me now. You need me to get in—that backdoor access I told you about. Remember?"

"I'm not sure I do," Tiberius said. "You already told me where the access door is located."

"You need the code," the man said. "Otherwise it won't open."

"I can make you give me the code."

He made a clicking noise and the wolves raced over to the American. They stood, hackles raised, less than a foot away, barking and growling. Tiberius then lifted the whistle he kept on a cord to his lips.

The hostage cowered and shouted, "You need me to get into the safe. You need my help."

Tiberius frowned.

"I can just chop off Cryer's head and hold it up to the retinal scan or whatever fancy keypad he has installed," he said, but kept the hand with his whistle hovering near his lips.

"It's next level. It measures biometrics. It will take into account the person's body temperature. If Cryer is dead, it won't work."

"You think you're going to be better at talking your boss into opening it than I will be?"

The man shrugged and said, "I might know how to bypass it."

The wolf handler had been observing the man's body language the entire time and knew that, up until this moment, the man had been telling the truth. But now he was lying. He had no way to bypass the access panel to a safe. The wolf handler kept his lips pressed tightly together. This was not his concern.

The wolves remained in front of the hostage, snarling and snapping at him.

The handler knew that one note from Tiberius's whistle would trigger the attack.

Tiberius stared at the American for a long moment.

Then the rebel warlord nodded.

"Then it looks like your usefulness will allow you to live another day," he said. "But you must know you are simply postponing the inevitable."

17

Without waiting for anyone to answer their knock, Lucky and Shepherd stormed into Cryer's suite.

"Hey!" Cryer jumped up from his leather chair, sloshing some of the vodka out of his crystal tumbler.

The Darcy brothers had drawn their weapons but lowered them when they saw who it was.

"Oh, it's the dynamic duo," Connor Darcy said.

Lucky shrugged. "Better than being Tweedledee and Tweedledum."

Cryer's face was red. "You have some nerve barging in here," he said. "My men told me the situation and what happened at the meet. Do you realize you knuckleheads started World War III on my turf!"

A tiny bit of spittle flew out of his mouth as he yelled.

"Your men?" Lucky winked at Clint, who made a face at her.

"You've ruined everything," Cryer continued. "If that hostage is dead, it's on your head. We were making the exchange. Everything was going along as planned."

"Your plan sucked," Lucky said, and strode over to the bar near the window.

She plopped two ice cubes in a crystal glass and then looked at

Shepherd. He shook his head. She poured some of the tonic water into the glass and downed it while Cryer watched with his mouth open.

She sat down on the edge of his desk and swung one steel-toe boot. He narrowed his eyes. "My plan didn't involve provoking the rebel leader into attacking my factory! I wonder what your boss thinks of that."

"I wonder, too," Lucky said. "We can't exactly reach him. Our phones are dead. Maybe we could call from your line?"

She nodded at an old-fashioned desk phone.

"It's just for looks," Lockwood said. "I also have tried to reach your employer to explain what happened, but all the cell signals are down because of the incoming storm."

He turned toward the floor-to-ceiling windows.

The rest did as well.

In the distance, dark, roiling clouds were gathering. Massive orange lights, like those found in a harbor, now lit up the compound below.

The setting sun was completely obliterated, and small, jagged silver bolts shot across the sky every few seconds. As if on cue, a terrific boom rocked the windows and made the crystal glasses on their mirrored bar titter.

Shepherd raised an eyebrow. Lucky frowned.

"I hate thunder," she said. Her brow was furrowed.

"I can't believe I didn't know this," Shepherd said. "All this time and there actually is something that rattles you."

"I'm not rattled," she said, but hopped off the desk away from the window. "Anyway, why is there thunder? It's snowing, not raining."

"Snow thunder," Cryer said. "We see this on the ranch in Montana. Unfortunately it's not going to keep a rebel warlord away."

"What's the deal with the phones?" Clint Darcy asked.

"The heavy cloud cover is blocking the signal for the phones," Lockwood said. "We are not in Kansas anymore, folks."

"Thanks for the tip," Lucky said dryly.

"That's not acceptable," Shepherd said. "We need helicopters inbound immediately."

"I've already tried to arrange that," Lockwood said. "There's no way a helicopter will fly in this weather."

The wind began to wail. The windows groaned as gale-force winds pelted them. The dark mass of swirling clouds was whipping closer.

"We'll have whiteout conditions within the next hour," Cryer said. "Nobody is going anywhere."

"We still need to be prepared to evacuate," Shepherd said. "The second the sky clears, we move."

"What about your employees?" Lucky asked. "How many people are in the apartments across the way? We need a total number."

Lockwood and Cryer exchanged a look.

"So?" Lucky raised an eyebrow.

"Most were released for the week to celebrate Mawlid with their families. It's a big holiday so I'm not sure if anyone is still over there. We essentially shut down the offices and plant for the week," Lockwood said.

"So you don't have a count of the ones who remain? You don't know who is here or what apartments they are in? What floors?"

"What are your evacuation plans for your employees who are on campus?" Shepherd asked Cryer.

Cryer looked at Lockwood.

He remained expressionless.

"Well?" Lucky said.

Cryer raised an eyebrow.

"Sorry," Lockwood said lightly. "Guess you'll have to go door to door."

Lucky scowled, then turned toward the Darcy brothers.

"What about you two?"

Clint shook his head. "That's not our problem. We were hired—and paid, I might add—to protect Paxton Cryer. The employees are on their own. Plus they won't be targeted anyway."

Lucky scoffed. "The hell they won't. They'll be taken out just for the fun of it. The rebels don't care about collateral damage. Weren't you there earlier today, or do you have another twin brother who stood in for you?"

The two brothers exchanged a startled look.

Lucky was growing frustrated. "But seriously? You think the employees are safe with these animals? Have you watched the news?"

Clint frowned at her. "I don't watch the news. It's a waste of time."

"Well here's a newsflash for you—we leave without them and they're dead," she said.

"Oh, come on," Connor said. "Don't tell me you've never had an op where you had to triage and decide who lives or who dies? That's the way it works, girlie."

Lucky was behind him in less than a second. She bladed her right palm and slid it along his neck, under his chin, and then up the other side of his head so her elbow encircled his jaw before he even knew what hit him. With the same hand, she clutched her left bicep. She bent her left arm and cupped the back of his head, holding it firm. She pulled her shoulders back.

Her movement had taken him off guard, but not his brother, who had the barrel of a gun on the back of Lucky's head the second she made contact.

Shepherd was right behind him with the barrel of his weapon pressed into the other brother's ribcage. "Easy now," Shepherd hissed into Clint's ear.

Connor's eyes were bulging and he frantically tapped her elbow. She released her grip slightly and smiled.

"It's cool," Lucky said. "Just giving him a warning."

Connor grinned. "I can feel your heart beating, g—" She tightened her grip and his eyes bulged.

"Call me girlie again and I'll break your neck before your brother can squeeze the trigger. Trust me, it will be worth it."

Clint grinned. "Sounds fair."

Lucky released her chokehold and stepped back. Connor stepped back too, and Shepherd put his gun away.

"That was a smooth move," he said, smiling at Lucky.

"Bas Rutten's rear naked choke," she said.

"Will you four quit acting like kindergarteners and do your job?" Cryer said. "For Christ's sake."

Shepherd strode toward the door.

"We're not leaving anyone behind," he said.

Lucky followed him and said in a low voice, "Don't worry. It won't be like Ramadi, I promise. I'm with you all the way. We don't leave anyone behind."

He nodded and said quietly, "Thanks."

She squeezed his arm and then they moved apart.

"None of that matters, anyway," Cryer said. "There aren't going to be any helicopters coming in anytime soon. Trust me."

"A storm isn't going to stop Tiberius," Shepherd said. "That guy will be here, come hell or high water."

"Facts," Lucky said, and opened the door to the suite. "In the meantime, let's go next door and gather up the civilians. We can move them to an upper floor and secure the area. Do you have any conference rooms or big spaces in that building?"

Lucky's question was met by silence.

"Yo," she said, and took a few steps toward Cryer.

Clint Darcy stepped in front of her before she could touch him. He grinned down at her.

"Calm down," she barked, and he stepped aside.

"I asked you a question," she said, standing in front of Cryer. "Do you have any big spaces in the other building on the upper floors?"

He blinked, and then sighed. "I honestly don't know."

"What do you mean, you don't know?" Shepherd said.

"I've never been over there."

"Wow." Lucky shook her head, then turned toward Lockwood. "You must know."

"I don't," he said. "But I can look at the blueprints."

He pulled up a document on his phone.

"There is a small meeting room on the top floor."

"Thank you," Lucky said.

Shepherd started toward the door and then turned toward the Darcy brothers. "It would go a lot faster if we all worked together. Once we get everyone secured, we can make a plan to defend this place."

Clint laughed.

"Dude, if you want to be a hero, get on with your bad self. We're staying here. Our op was to protect these two. My understanding was you were supposed to look after shorty here," he said, pointing to Mako. "But maybe you guys don't like to follow the rules."

Connor stopped forward.

"We'll all be waiting over here in the CEO quarters, with a bird's-eye view of anyone trying to attack. We'll probably have a nice meal, maybe drink some of this expensive vodka. You all go on and be heroes. We'll wait here. Good luck."

18

Pete Brody looked around the small apartment and tried to find something cheerful about it. Anything.

It only had two bedrooms. Which was the biggest problem for the kids right now. They were screaming at each other and Pete and Liz about being way too old to share a room. And frankly, they were right.

"Wait!" Pete said in an excited voice. "This living room area has doors and the couch is a fold-out bed. Your mom and I can sleep here and you guys can each have one of the bedrooms! Problem solved!"

Liz, who was opening cupboard doors and making faces, turned and shook her head, as if she was disgusted.

"It will be fine," Pete said. "We like to stay up late and watch TV anyway so it will work out fine, right, honey?"

"Sure, Pete," Liz answered in a resigned monotone. She opened the refrigerator door and recoiled. A foul smell filled the air.

"Oh my God. This milk is soured. I can't even imagine how long it's been here."

"I got it!" Pete rushed over to grab the milk. "Be right back."

And he was gone.

He let the door close behind him. Standing in the hall, he leaned back against the door, closing his eyes. This was a disaster. His eyes snapped open. He reeled from the smell of the milk and held it at arm's length.

He gave himself a small pep talk as he walked down the hall. *It will get better.* He wasn't sure what to do with the milk so he walked to the end of the hall and opened the door to the stairs. He looked around and then set the putrid carton in a corner of the stairwell. He'd figure out what to do with it later.

Meanwhile, he had bigger things to worry about. He only had a small window of time to convince Cryer of his idea to use the factory's tunnels to convert and transport fresh water to the nearby village. It would change lives. He had waited his entire life to do something meaningful that would help others. This was his chance. He wasn't going to let these housing difficulties stand in his way.

As he walked back to his apartment, he realized that the hallway was eerily quiet.

On a whim, he knocked on one door. No answer. He held his ear to the door and knocked again. There was no noise from inside.

Following a hunch, he rapped on each door he passed as he walked back to his place. Nobody answered. It was creepy and made him uneasy. What had he gotten himself—and his family—into?

Pausing in front of his apartment door, he took a deep breath and told himself, "You got this, Brody!"

He walked in with a big smile.

"Hey, I think we're the only ones on the floor this week ... that holiday—"

As he spoke, the lights went out.

"You've got to be kidding," Liz said.

"Daddy, I'm scared," Will said.

"This is the stupidest place on earth," Cassidy added.

"Hold on." Pete opened the door to the hall. The light was out there, too. "I'm sure it will be back on—"

He hadn't finished speaking when the lights flickered back on.

For a second, it looked like his entire family had rolled their eyes at him, but he wasn't sure.

"I hate this place!" Will stormed into a bedroom, slamming the door behind him.

"For once I agree with the little brat," Cassidy said, and then she too was gone.

Liz closed her eyes for a brief second and put her hand to her head.

"You okay?" he said.

"I'll be fine." Her lips were pressed tightly together.

"I'm going to find the plant engineer and see what we're dealing with as far as the tunnels," Pete said. "If I get the engineer on board, we can convince Cryer that this can change lives."

"You're going to do that now?"

Pete frowned and looked at his watch.

"Yeah, I think I need to. Dinner is in an hour. I need to have some ammo when I sit down with him."

He opened the door.

"Pete, I'm sure Mr. Cryer is going to be open to what you have to say. Didn't they say they brought you on because of your reputation as a guy who can take anything and make it environmentally friendly? They pointed out that article that was in the newspaper last year. Didn't they call you the Green Guy in that one interview?"

Pete grinned. "Yeah. Yeah, they did. But I still need to have a strong argument. Back soon."

Once he got to the ground floor, Pete found a back door out of the building that led to the factory that would shorten the walk, which wasn't that bad to begin with, but every minute counted. He was in a hurry.

The wind was whipping and he regretted not wearing his coat as he leaned into it, keeping his head down as he walked toward the factory. A huge gust of wind made him look up, and he saw a thick layer of heavy, roiling black clouds forming above him.

Then he was at the plant's front door. He yanked it open and rushed inside.

The interior was dim. There were a few lights down the hall. He walked toward them.

"Hello?" he yelled. "Anyone here?"

As he walked, he looked around. He realized that he was traveling a narrow path through towering piles of plastic stacked high in huge roll-off trailers.

He stopped and backtracked, then went down another aisle. Same thing. Soon, he'd stood at the edge of ten identical tunnels that seemed to stretch all the way to the factory's back wall.

Instead of a recycling facility with humming equipment to recycle the plastic, he stood in a storage room—a giant warehouse full of plastic stacked in cubes.

He stopped and scratched his head. He'd studied the blueprints every day from the minute he'd been offered the job. This didn't make sense. He took out the blueprints again. Looking at them, he headed to the farthest corner of the factory. There, he found the door he'd been looking for. A forklift was parked in front of it, but he squeezed behind it.

He cracked the door. A dank, musty scent floated out on a cool breeze. The door to the tunnel. He heard skittering. Then he heard another sound behind him. He quickly and quietly shut the door and stepped out from behind the forklift.

He wasn't sure why he felt he had to be secretive about what he was doing, as if he'd been caught doing something wrong.

Maybe just because he was caught snooping on his own. It was silly. He worked here, too.

"Anyone here?" someone called from further down the back wall.

"Hello?" he hollered. "I'm looking for the plant engineer."

"Who are you?"

"Pete Brody. I'm the new engineer."

He followed the voice. A few seconds later, a face emerged out of the dim light.

The man was older with thinning hair and a craggy face. He wore faded blue coveralls and was smoking a cigarette.

"New engineer, huh?" the man said.

"Yes, sir." The man seemed a bit standoffish so Pete dropped the hand he had held out for him to shake.

"Nobody told me nothing about a new engineer." The man frowned.

"Well, I think that was an oversight," Pete said. "It seems like you're the one in charge of this warehouse."

"Warehouse?" The man scratched his head. That was when Pete saw a name embroidered on the coverall.

"Hey, Tom. It's nice to meet you, but I think I'm lost," Pete said. "I must be looking at an old blueprint. It shows that this is where the recycling facility is but clearly this is just a storehouse."

The man blinked but didn't answer.

"Tom? Where is the actual recycling facility?"

"The what?"

"The place where all this plastic is recycled."

Tom shook his head sadly.

"Son, this is it."

"What?" Pete's face scrunched up in confusion.

"This is all there is."

"That can't be," Pete said. "What about through that door there? Is there another section I'm missing?"

The two men sat in silence.

There were no machines cranking away. There wasn't anything except huge roll-off containers piled high with plastic.

Plastic for as far as he could see. Reds, blues, yellows, purples, browns, oranges. Plastic everywhere.

And no machines. No machines to recycle the plastic.

It still didn't compute, so Pete tried again.

"I don't understand," he said. "Where is the other part of the plant?"

"There ain't no other part of the plant." Tom scratched his head again.

"What do you do with all this plastic? What are the roll-off containers and trucks for? Where do they go?"

Pete rarely got angry, but he realized he had raised his voice.

Finally, after taking a long drag off his cigarette, Tom shook his head. "How much about this place did they tell you?"

"That it was a recycling plant for plastics."

Tom eyed the rolled-up blueprint. "They give you that?"

Pete shook his head. "No, I found it on my own. I was trying to, I don't know, impress the CEO with my knowledge, and I found these tunnels and I had this idea for fresh water for the village..."

He trailed off.

"This isn't a recycling plant, is it?"

The man shook his head sadly.

"You poor sap. How'd they convince you to come all the way over here?"

"What? I don't understand." Pete's voice was now high-pitched and strained.

"Come see for yourself."

Tom walked past a small golf cart parked in the opposite corner. He punched in some numbers and then stuck his eye to a retinal scan.

"Only about three of us have access to open this door," Tom said as a huge steel door slid open. "And the other two are missing. But I think this is something you need to see."

After the door opened, Pete walked over and stood in front of it. When he saw what was beyond the door, he froze. His knees buckled.

The door opened up to a narrow roadway that wound about a mile to a burning pile of plastic in the distance.

Huge curls of black smoke rose into the air.

"No!" he said. "You've got to be kidding?"

He whipped his head toward Tom, who had lit another cigarette. After exhaling and shaking his match out, Tom spoke again.

"I've got to close this now. I'm only allowed to open it every twelve hours when we got a driver to take the roll-offs over there and dump them. But our driver is with his family celebrating some Islamic holiday so we aren't transporting any plastic this week. It's fine, though. That fire never goes out. Even with the storm coming in, it will keep burning."

"This is... this is," Pete spluttered, and shook his head. "This is unbelievable."

"Sorry, pal, I guess they weren't real clear about what we do over here, were they?"

Pete shook his head and began to leave. His shoulders were slumped and his mouth was dry.

The other man was shouting something after him, but he couldn't hear it. All he heard was a buzzing in his head.

By the time he reached the door, he squared his shoulders and held his head high. He was going to find Cryer. He was going to find him and give him a piece of his mind. And then he was going to ...

He wasn't sure what he would do after that, but it was not going to be pretty.

As he walked back to his building, he looked up at the skyway connecting it to the executive offices. He'd take the skyway and go visit Cryer before dinner. He couldn't face his family right then. After stepping into the elevator in his building, he punched the button for the skyway, his blood boiling.

He was about to give Paxton Cryer a piece of his mind.

19

In the elevator going down to the lobby of the CEO's high-rise building, Shepherd was fuming.

"Those arrogant bastards are going to get everyone killed."

"I think that's exactly what Cryer said about us," Lucky said lightly.

He glowered at her.

"They don't care about anyone but themselves."

Lucky gave him a long look. She knew exactly why he was so upset.

"It's not going to be the same. It won't be like that."

"How do you know?" He crossed his arms.

"I promise you I won't let that happen. Between the two of us, we will make sure nobody is left behind."

He looked at her, exhaled, and gave a small smile. She smiled back.

He took a step closer. It seemed like they were both holding their breath.

"Adam, I'm not going to ever let innocent civilians die again if I can help it. You know that." Her voice was husky with desire.

"Thanks for always having my back," he said, and the rumble of his voice sent a thrill down her spine.

"It's not a bad back to have," she murmured.

He reached over to tuck a loose strand of hair off her face. Within lightning-like reflexes, she snatched his hand by the wrist and was about to twist it when he stepped closer. They were both breathing heavily. He lowered his face to hers and kissed her—softly at first and then more urgently.

She pressed her body to his and let out a small groan.

He reached for the buttons on the elevator. He paused with his finger hovering over the emergency stop button.

"We can't," she said.

With his hand tangled in her hair, he pressed his forehead to hers. "I know. I know."

"Let's go find those workers. What if the extraction team comes before we're ready? What if they leave without them?"

They drew back from one another, but before they did, Shepherd ran his thumb across her lips. "I'm not going to let that happen," he said in a soft voice.

Exhaling loudly, Lucky nodded.

"You know you're the only person in this world I can always count on."

"Hey!" a voice said. "What about me?"

They both jumped.

It was Red on Shepherd's wrist comm.

"Red! Can you hear us?" Shepherd said.

"You're coming in faint and staticky but I can hear. I got your message. We're trying to get helos in asap but there's a mother of a storm coming."

"What's the ETA?"

Silence.

"Red? You still there?"

"We...dangerous...as soon as possible...stay put."

The words were broken and fuzzy.

"Stay put?" Lucky echoed.

Shepherd shook his head. He held his wrist up to his face even though he knew it wouldn't make a difference. "Red, if you can hear us, this place is a fortress, but I'm not a hundred percent convinced that

Tiberius can't get through. Send help asap. We've got civilians on site with families."

"Kids!" Lucky said loudly. "We've got families with kids."

There was nothing but silence on the other end as the elevator doors opened into the lobby.

Two guards sat behind a large desk with their heads bowed over what looked like iPads.

"Wake up, fellas," Lucky said. "Game time. We're about to be attacked and we need your help locking down this front entrance."

"What?" a guard with a red beard and crew cut said. "Who are you?"

"Private security hired by the owner of this joint," Shepherd said.

"That's our job," said the other guy. He was muscular and good-looking with a chiseled jaw and floppy bangs.

"Okay," Shepherd said, "we're actually mercenaries. They brought us in as protection for the big kahunas around here. But right now all you need to know is we're in charge."

The muscled guy's face drained of color.

The redhead frowned. "This whole place can be locked up tighter than Fort Knox. Watch."

He hit a button and a thick metal wall came down in front of the building's small glass entryway.

"Nice," Lucky said.

"There aren't any other windows on the first three levels," he said. "We're good to go. Even with an RPG they can't get through that metal door."

"What about the building that houses the workers?" Shepherd asked. "Same deal?"

"You mean where we live?" the muscled guard scoffed. "Hardly. You're on that side, you're screwed."

Lucky shook her head.

The redheaded guard stood and stretched. "It's not that bad," he said. "There's no way anybody is getting over that wall or through that front gate. One thing I'll say about Paxton Cryer is that no expense was spared when it came to security."

"Are there any other access points besides that front gate?" Shepherd asked.

The two guards exchanged a look.

"Well?" Lucky said.

"There is a maintenance door at the back of the factory," the redhead said. "It's an access door to transport the roll-off containers to the burning field."

Lucky and Shepherd exchanged a look.

"Are armed guards stationed there?" Shepherd asked.

The redhead shook his head. "But it's a solid steel garage door armed with a digital lock and retinal scan. Only the top personnel have the codes. We don't even know how to open those doors."

"Let us out and then lock down this building again," Lucky said. "Is there a way for us to contact you if we need to come back in this way?"

The redhead shook his head. "Not unless you have a radio."

"Got a spare one?" Shepherd asked.

The muscled guard shook his head.

"You can use the skyway from the employee housing building," the other man said. "Your keycard will work to get in there and through the skyway to most of the floors."

"Got it," Shepherd said as the metal doors lifted.

As he and Lucky stepped into the executive building's closed glass foyer, the metal doors slammed shut behind them. Through the set of glass doors behind them they saw the storm had arrived.

Wind whipped the snow, creating a whiteout condition. They couldn't even see the employee building across the way.

"You ready?" Shepherd asked.

"Yeah. Let's do this."

They ran across the street to the other building and raced inside the lobby.

"We're going to have to go floor to floor," Lucky said as she looked at the map detailing the building's emergency escape route.

"No better time than now."

They raced up the stairs. On the first two floors, nobody answered the door even though they knocked, rang doorbells, and shouted in the halls.

On the third floor, a man opened the door. He was heavyset with a beard and bloodshot eyes and was holding a bottle of whiskey by the neck. He yawned, said something in Russian, and went back inside.

Lucky pounded until he answered again. She pointed toward the elevator and then made her finger into a gun and pointed it at him.

"You have to leave."

He looked at her blankly.

"Tiberius is coming," Shepherd said.

The man's face blanched at the name. He withdrew and tried to slam the door. Shepherd stuck his steel-toe boot in the gap and said, "Come with us."

The man shook his head. "Go!"

"Listen, pal, do you speak English? Tiberius is coming and he's going to kill everyone."

"He won't kill me." The man reached behind the door and pulled out an assault rifle.

Shepherd backed up, holding out his palms.

"Easy now."

The man slammed the door.

Lucky pulled on Shepherd's arm. "We can't make him come with us."

Reluctantly, he drew back and muttered, "At least he'll have a fighting chance. For a few seconds."

On the fourth floor, nobody answered any of the doors again.

"Do you think they're hiding from us or are all the employees actually on that holiday right now?" Lucky asked.

"I'm hoping they're all far away from here."

"Same."

On the sixth floor, a woman who looked like she was in her twenties opened the door.

Lucky plastered a smile on her face even though she felt frantic. "Hi, do you speak English? We work for the owner of the factory and we've been told to evacuate the building."

The woman frowned. "Evacuate? I don't understand."

"You're in danger if you stay."

The woman started to close the door. "I don't know who you are. My father is elderly. We can't just leave. We have no place to go."

Shepherd smiled. "I know it seems odd," he said. "I'm just asking you to trust us. The rebels are planning an attack on this compound. We were told to get everyone to safety. If you could just pack a small bag and come with us, we have helicopters that will fly us to a safe spot."

"Do we get to come back?" the woman asked.

"I don't know," Lucky said.

"The rebels?"

"Tiberius," Shepherd said.

The name provoked the same response as with the Russian-speaking man. The woman's face drained of color. "He is coming here? Why?"

"Long story. We're here to keep you safe."

She looked at Shepherd for a long moment and then nodded.

"Give us five minutes."

The door shut.

Lucky raised her eyebrow. "Well, that was easy."

"We'll see."

But five minutes later, the door opened. This time an older man stood behind the woman.

"I'm Nadia. This is my father, Ahmed Nazir."

"Nice to meet you, Nadia and Mr. Nazir. My name is Lucky."

"Adam Shepherd."

They both nodded.

"We're going to head to the skyway and then over to the office building. That building seems, uh, slightly more fortified than this one. I think we're safer there, and that's where the helipad is," Shepherd said.

"Okay."

"Do you know if any other employees are in the building? It seems sort of empty," Lucky said.

The woman shook her head. "They shut the plant down entirely for this week so everyone could go home for Mawlid. We stayed. We don't have any other family."

The father nodded sadly.

The four of them stepped into the elevator.

As they stepped out on the seventh floor, they could hear loud music playing.

"Maybe everyone's up here?" Lucky said.

They knocked on doors, saving the one with the music behind it for last.

Nobody answered any of their knocks or shouts until they all stood in front of number 723.

The sounds of Marvin Gaye's "Ain't No Mountain High Enough" blared from the apartment.

Shepherd knocked a few times before the music shut off.

"Who is it?" a woman called.

"Ma'am, we work for the company and need to speak to you."

A few seconds later the door opened.

The woman stood with her hands on her hips.

She said something in Russian.

Lucky spoke up. "Do you speak English?"

The woman flushed. "I'm sorry. Can I help you?"

"You're American?" Shepherd asked.

"Yes, I'm Elizabeth Brody. Sorry about the music. My husband said we were the only ones on the floor this week ... the music is for my teenage daughter ... We just moved here and I'm trying to cheer her up." She smiled. "What's going on?"

"We need to evacuate. There is a threat on the factory compound. We are here to help facilitate the evacuation."

"What?" the woman said, her mouth dropping open.

Just then a door slammed open. "Why'd you turn off the music?"

A teenage girl in an oversized sweatshirt and leggings stepped out. A second later, a boy who looked about ten emerged from another room.

"Mom, I'm hungry—" His words cut off when he saw the group in the doorway.

"I don't understand," Elizabeth Brody said. "My husband and I just arrived earlier today. He's starting his new job ... we're having dinner with the CEO tonight. In a few hours, I think."

Lucky shook her head. "We'll explain later. Right now we need to get you over to the other building where the helipad is. We're going to evacuate with helicopters as soon as the weather clears. I need you all in position for when that window opens up."

"What window is opening?" the boy said.

"What she means," Shepherd said, "is that as soon as the storm calms down enough, a helicopter is coming to fly us to the border."

"A helicopter?" the boy said. "Cool."

"This is crazy!" the woman said. "My husband's not even here. He went to tour the factory."

Lucky frowned.

"We'll go get him," Shepherd said.

As soon as the words came out of his mouth, the lights flickered and then went out.

"It's been doing that all afternoon," the woman said. "It usually comes back on after a few seconds."

They all sat there in the dark.

"Mom, we can use my phone," the girl said.

"Good idea, honey."

"I want Dad," the boy said.

Lucky had turned on her phone flashlight as well. She now shined it on the family standing before her.

"We're going to get your dad and then all of us will meet together upstairs near where the helicopter is landing, across the skyway, okay?"

The teenage girl bit her lip and nodded, but the boy backed up and shouted, "No! No! I'm not going across that death trap. Are you kidding? With the wind and snow it's just going to collapse."

"Will!" his mother said.

"Mom, you can't make me."

"Mrs. Brody, would you be able to lead your family and Nadia and Ahmed Nazir up to the skyway level of the building? We'll go find your husband and meet you there in a few minutes."

"Yes," she said. Her voice was shaking. "Give me a few minutes to pack."

"You speak Russian?" Shepherd said.

"Barely," the mother said.

"I barely speak English," Nadia said, and smiled.

"Perfect," the mother said. "Between the two of us we'll figure it out."

"Not to interrupt, but we don't have time," Lucky said. "We need you to leave now."

"I'll be quick. Everything is still packed."

"I'm not leaving," the boy said, crossing his arms over his chest.

"Will," the girl said. "We need to go meet Daddy."

"I'm not leaving without Joey."

"That's fine." The mother shot a glance over her son's head at Lucky. "He can fit in your backpack. Go get him. I'll be there in a second."

As soon as the boy ran out of the room, the woman turned back.

"Go. I'll handle this on our end. I'll lead everyone upstairs. Just go get my husband. Please."

Lucky and Shepherd headed to the elevators but immediately realized that they were inoperable with the power out.

Shepherd ran back to the open door.

"You're going to take the stairs. It's only two floors up. We'll meet you there asap. Everything's going to be just fine."

And then he and Lucky headed for the stairwell.

As they took the stairs down two at a time, Lucky said, "You lied."

"About what?" Shepherd said.

"Everything being just fine."

Pressing his lips together, Shepherd didn't answer.

20

It took a hell of a lot to make Pete Brody angry.

It also took a lot to crush his spirit.

But that spirit was hanging by a thread as he marched through the CEO building looking for Cryer's office.

The stomping out of his dream to create a freshwater source at the factory was just a small blow compared to the realization that he had uprooted his entire life and family to work for a man who was actually destroying the environment. Not to mention the lives of people who lived nearby with the toxic scum he was releasing by burning the plastic.

Pete was fuming. When he looked at his reflection in a window he was passing, he was surprised he didn't have steam coming out his ears.

His fists were clenched and he stomped along, feeling his face hot with anger.

Finally, he saw the door to Cryer's office.

Without stopping to take a breath or knock, he swiped his keycard and barged in.

As he stepped into the room, he saw that the hallway was flanked by two smaller offices with glass walls. But he kept his sights focused on the large wooden door straight in front of him that said "Paxton Cryer" on it.

As he stormed past one of the offices, he happened to glance over.

A woman was sitting at a desk with papers spread out over the surface. Her head was down and she was taking notes.

A second later, he charged into Paxton Cryer's suite, waving the blueprints in his hand.

"I just toured your so-called factory!" he shouted. "This isn't a recycling plant! This is an abomination."

Paxton Cryer was unruffled by Pete's anger.

"Would you care for a drink?" He turned his back on Pete and used tongs to retrieve ice cubes out of a silver ice bucket.

"No! I don't want a drink!" Pete said. "I want to know what's going on here and why you lied to me and how you could live with yourself doing something this ... this ... evil."

"Evil is a pretty strong word." Cryer turned around. He took a sip of his drink and studied Pete for the first time. "My dear friend, it's all in your perspective. In reality, we're actually doing the world a favor. Nobody except me had the balls to figure out what really needed to happen with all this plastic. If it wasn't for us taking it off the world's hands, it would be polluting landfills, rivers, lakes, oceans, you name it. We were the only ones who had the brains to just burn it. I mean, it's a little smoke in the ozone. In comparison to everything else we are doing to destroy the ozone, it's a drop of water in the ocean."

"You're insane," Pete said.

"They said the same thing about Isaac Newton."

Pete shook his head and marched over to the big walnut desk, unfurling the blueprint he was still carrying.

"Look at this blueprint. With the tunnels, it had so much potential. I had plans to build a freshwater source using the recycling plant. But now, with what you've done, I'd have to start from scratch. We have to stop this. It's atrocious."

Pete began to pace. That was when he noticed that the woman in the glass office had stopped what she was doing to stare at him.

Cryer turned his head to see what Pete was looking at. As soon as he did, he sputtered, "Jesus Christ. Let's take this into my suite."

21

Lucky and Shepherd ran through the biting wind and snow flurries and flung open the door to the plant. Slamming the door behind them, they paused to catch their breath.

Shepherd looked around and then yelled, "Brody? Pete Brody?"

His voice echoed in the cavernous space.

"This way." Lucky began to run down a narrow, dimly lit walkway toward light at the other end.

When they got there, they found a small office with windows. An older man with thinning hair and blue coveralls jumped up from a desk when he saw them.

"We're looking for Pete Brody," Shepherd said.

"New guy? Yeah. He left here a few minutes ago." The man's eyebrows knit together. "What's going on?"

"We're evacuating the compound. You're going to need to come with us."

"Why? What's going on?" The man put his hands on his hips, spread his feet, and gave them a suspicious look.

"A rebel warlord has declared war on this place."

"Tiberius?"

"The very same."

The man shook his head. "Damn fools. They should have never poked the sleeping dragon."

"Let's get you out of here," Shepherd said.

"First show us the back access gate," Lucky said.

"I can't open it. I already opened it earlier to show the new kid. It's programmed to only let me open it once every twelve hours. For security."

"Just show us."

He led them over to a massive steel garage door.

Lucky flipped the cover on the access panel and examined it for a few seconds. Then she shut it.

"If you can't open it, I know it's secure," Shepherd said.

"What are you, some kind of model who has a side gig as a burglar?" the man asked Lucky.

"Something like that," she said, and winked.

"You need to get to the CEO offices now. We're going to evacuate by helicopter," Shepherd said.

The man grumbled and grabbed a lunch box from the desk before turning off the lights. "All the same to me."

They started back the way they came but he began walking another way.

"Where you going, pal?" Shepherd said.

"I'm not going out in that blizzard," he said. "Follow me. This side of the building has direct access to the executive suites. If you have the right access guard."

He held up a keycard. "The average yahoos have to go back through the employee building, but if we're going to the helipad this will be the fastest way."

Lucky raised an eyebrow. "Sounds good to me."

They walked through the factory until they reached a thick, reinforced steel door with a keypad next to it.

"Looks like the two guards forgot to tell us about this door," Shepherd said.

"The two meatheads at the front desk?" the man asked. "Bozos."

The man swiped a keycard and the door opened.

They stepped inside a narrow hallway with two doors and an elevator. One door said "utilities" and the other "basement."

Shepherd punched the up button on the elevator.

It opened immediately. A mop and bucket were propped in one corner.

It was a service elevator.

"I'm going to get off on the fourth floor," the man said. "I got something I need to grab there."

"As soon as the helicopter touches down, we're out of here," Lucky said. "Why don't you leave whatever you want behind and come straight up with us."

"It's the only photo of my dead wife," the man said as the elevator stopped on the fourth floor. "It's on my other desk. I was just filling in during Mawlid down there. I'm not leaving without Corrine so don't even try to stop me. I'll take the stairs too. You don't need to wait for me."

He stepped out of the elevator and was gone.

"We don't have time to wait for him anyway," Shepherd said. "We've got to get Mako."

When the elevator stopped on the floor for the executive offices and slid open, a man with blond hair and a ruddy face stood facing them. He was swearing to himself and running a hand through his hair, making it stand on end.

"Pete Brody?" Shepherd asked, raising an eyebrow.

"Yeah, who's asking?"

"Easy now," Lucky said.

"God, I'm sorry," Pete said. "I'm just having a bad day. Maybe the worst day ever. Have you ever had all your dreams crumble in a few minutes?"

"Where's your family?" Lucky looked at the stairway leading to the floors below. She knew the skyway level was two floors down.

He shrugged. "I'm assuming they are still in our cruddy little apartment trying to make the best of it."

Lucky and Shepherd exchanged a glance.

"We're evacuating," Shepherd said quickly. "Your wife was rounding everybody up to bring them to this side. She was supposed to take the skyway. She should be here by now."

Before he'd even finished speaking, Pete had dropped a large bundle of blueprints and sprinted for the stairwell door.

"Should we go help?" Lucky asked.

"We've got to get Mako."

"Hurry!" she yelled after Pete right before the door swung shut behind him. "Meet us back here."

22

After witnessing the blond man confronting Paxton Cryer, Mako knew that something much bigger than an accounting discrepancy was in play.

While she didn't hear every word of the argument, she heard enough.

Words such as "evil" and "abomination" and the fact that there actually wasn't any recycling being done.

Mako lifted her forearm and spoke into her wrist comm.

"Max? You there?"

"What's up? Just finished up my meeting with NextLife."

"Oh, God," Mako said. "You're not really going to do that, are you?"

"Yup," Max said. "After I die my brain is going to be uploaded to the cloud. Just think, you'll be one of the few people who can access it."

"Lucky me."

"Do I sense reluctance?"

"Max, it's a bunch of crap. They say 'high-tech embalming?' What does that even mean?"

"Mako, you know I trust you implicitly in all things—at least when it comes to how I spend my money—but we're going to have to disagree on this one. If I have a chance to be immortal, even as a simulation, I'm taking that chance."

"Fine." She shook her head even though she knew he couldn't see it. "We got bigger problems here."

"I heard from Red. I've got Suni working on the extraction. The second the weather allows, the helicopters will be en route."

"Good, that will solve the immediate problem, but something else is going on. This new engineer and Cryer just had a blow-out fight in front of me. Apparently, there is no recycling going on at this recycling factory."

Max let out a long, low groan. "Once again I'm funding something that is nefarious? Is there anything out there I've given money to that does the world any good?"

"I'll let you know when I find something like that," she said. "Don't beat yourself up too badly. Hey, that's why you hired me, right? To fix all this. We'll figure this out. But Paxton Cryer has to go. We'll get him off site with the other evacuees, and he'll just never come back."

"Your instincts are always spot-on," Max said. "You knew something was fishy about that place."

"Yeah, yeah. So I'm good at my job, but that's not going to help when this rebel warlord shows up with his army and we're stuck here."

"That compound is well-fortified. It should stave them off until the weather clears."

"'Should' is the operative word."

"I'm doing everything I can to get the three of you out of there."

"We have to evacuate families here as well."

"Good Lord," Max said. "How many?"

"No idea. Shepherd and the Fox are on it right now."

"Wait," Max said. "They're your security detail. They're supposed to be with you."

"Details."

"Are you safe?"

Mako looked over at Cryer's office door. Through a gap in the door, she could see the men still arguing. She could hear their voices faintly.

"Yeah. I'm good. Cryer isn't worried about me right now at all. I think he's more worried about saving his ass."

"You're a lifesaver, Mako."

"You can thank me by saving my life."

"Will do."

"Gotta go."

Mako disconnected quickly when the employee came storming out of the office. He tried to slam the door behind him, but it caught on something and bounced open, leaving the door cracked a few inches. He rushed past her to the door.

She looked down at her paperwork, pretending not to notice as Cryer stormed by. He flung open the door to the hall and screamed at the two bodyguards.

"Do not let anyone in here again unless it's Lockwood. Do you understand?"

Mako shrank into her seat in the corner as he stomped back into his office suite.

For a few seconds, Mako watched Cryer pace the room in front of the large window. Then he stepped out of sight.

Mako slipped off her heels, crept quietly to his door, and peeked inside.

What she saw astounded her.

Cryer had removed a large black-and-white photograph from the wall and set it on his desk. Now, he was pressing his face up to a large panel with flashing lights.

He stepped back and the entire wall adjacent to him slid open, revealing a small room lined with steel walls—a vault. Stacks of plastic-wrapped cash were set on a steel table toward the back of the vault. A large black velvet jewelry box took center stage in the middle of the table, surrounded by the money.

Mako could hear Cryer breathing rapidly as he approached the velvet box.

She watched as he opened the lid. A massive pear-shaped diamond was nestled in the center of the oversized box. He grabbed a small black leather duffel bag off the ground and put the velvet box inside. Then he placed a larger duffel bag on the table and began to stuff stacks of cash inside it.

A phone on his desk rang. As he turned to answer it, Mako ducked behind the door and turned to run.

Michael Lockwood stood facing her with a gun.

"I really wish you wouldn't have seen that."

Mako glared at him. "It's too late. I've already told Uncle Max everything."

"Not everything," he said lightly. "You might have called him earlier, but I've been watching you since you left the office. You haven't been speaking to anyone or sending any messages. Lucky for him, Uncle Max doesn't know about the money or diamond, and we're going to keep it that way."

"But I know."

"You're not a problem," he said.

The door opened and Cryer stood there.

His round face grew bright red when he saw Mako.

"And here I was going to let you go," he said. "But now I'm afraid we can't do that."

He tossed the black duffel bag onto his desk.

"I've cleared out the vault, Michael. She needs to be locked in there until we are safely out of here."

Then he turned to Mako.

"I wish I could say the door will open once we're miles away, but it won't."

He glanced down at her Apple watch.

"Even if you could call out or use that, these walls are impenetrable. No electronic signal. Nothing. You probably will have air for some time, but there won't be anyone to come rescue you—especially not your useless bodyguards who apparently abandoned you when the going got rough."

"They didn't abandon me, you jackass," Mako said. "They went to rescue your employees because you obviously don't care about anyone but yourself."

Cryer frowned at the name but then smiled. "Don't even try to escape. My handsome mug is the only thing that will open that vault, despite what my idiot employee apparently told Tiberius in a futile attempt to save his own life. Tiberius will try to get in the vault, but it's impossible. He's going to take this place over and you'll be counted as one of the rebel warlord's casualties. Unfortunately, it's not going to be a pleasant death—suffocation sounds awful. You should've just minded your own business."

Lockwood pushed Mako into the center of the vault and then stepped back.

"Why?" Mako stood in the center of the vault, arms crossed. "Why are you doing all this?"

"I did what I had to do."

23

When Shepherd and Lucky reached Paxton Cryer's offices, they were greeted by the twin bodyguards standing in front of the door.

"Move aside," Shepherd said.

"We were told nobody enters," Connor Darcy said.

"We don't care," Lucky said. "Our protectee is inside. Let us through."

"Not going to happen." Clint folded his arms across his chest and grinned.

"Wipe that smile off your face, soldier, and move aside." Lucky narrowed her eyes dangerously.

"You're feisty," Connor said.

"You have no idea," Shepherd snickered. "Now get out of our way before things get ugly."

"You threatening me?" Clint Darcy moved forward so he and Shepherd were facing off inches away from each other.

"Not a threat," Shepherd growled. "A promise."

Behind him, Lucky had squared off, ready to fight, when the door to Cryer's offices was flung open.

Clint Darcy stepped aside and Lockwood rushed out with a huge duffel bag in his hands. He looked like he was struggling to lift it.

Cryer was right behind him with a smaller duffle bag clutched to his chest.

The two men paused when they saw Lucky and Shepherd standing in the hall.

Lucky peered past them into the offices. The door to Cryer's private quarters was wide open.

"Where's Mako?" she asked.

Lockwood turned to face her. "No idea. Thought she was with you."

Cryer just looked past her as if she hadn't even spoken.

"Where you guys headed?" Shepherd folded his arms across his chest.

"We're heading to the roof, to the helipad," Lockwood said, stepping into the hall and letting the door slam shut behind him.

Cryer still hadn't said a word. A small bead of sweat dripped down his temple.

Lucky narrowed her eyes.

"Oh yeah?" she asked.

Nobody answered her.

"We're going to have some more people," Shepherd said. "If we count the families here and the remaining guards, I'd say a dozen. That's not counting the four of us." He poked a finger at the Darcy brothers and Lucky.

"Tell the pilot to wait to leave until we do a head count," Lucky said.

A slight smirk crossed Cryer's face.

Clint Darcy crossed his arms, matching Shepherd's posture.

"We're not going to be able to fit all those people," he said.

"You're going to have to." Lucky glared at him.

He pursed his lips and made a kissing noise.

Lucky started after him, but Shepherd grabbed her forearms.

"Later," he said in a low voice.

She relaxed.

A loud explosion rocked the building and the lights went out for a second. When they came back on, they were dim and flickering.

Everyone rushed to the large windows and peered down.

A convoy of huge military trucks was making its way toward the buildings from the front gate. Two trucks were already parked near the employee high rise. They heard another small explosion.

Shepherd nodded toward the elevator. The arrow showed it was moving up.

"They're in the building."

"If they're in the elevator, that means they already took out the lobby guards," Lucky said.

"We can expect them on the stairs as well," Connor Darcy said.

"What does this mean? Where is the helicopter?" Paxton Cryer's voice was frantic. He started to run toward the door to the rooftop stairwell.

"Hold up." Clint grabbed his collar. "We're making a plan."

Immediately after the words left his mouth, another explosion rocked the building and everything went black.

24

As the lights flickered back on, everyone ran to the windows and looked down.

"How did they get in?" Cryer asked.

"They are pouring out the factory doors. They breached the back access gate," Shepherd said.

"Impossible. Only a few people have that code."

"Is your hostage employee one of them?" Lucky asked.

Clint Darcy scoffed and shook his head.

"Drake wouldn't ..." Cryer began, and then cut off.

"You have wolves chomping at your junk, you'll do and say anything," Connor said.

"Facts," his brother added.

"Look," Shepherd said.

Rebel fighters were pouring out of the factory door, dressed in fatigues and armed with guns.

Lucky peered out. "There's too many. The convoy doesn't end. For as far as I can see."

"Look." Shepherd pointed in the distance.

"The helicopter."

It was weaving and dipping in the whipping wind and snow.

"Is it going to make it in?" Lucky asked.

"It better," Connor said, looking down at the vehicles filing into the compound. "They didn't spare any men when they came to visit."

"Can you see the skyway from there?" Shepherd asked Lucky.

"It's under us. I can't see through the roof and the sides are at a weird angle from here."

"Do we know if Pete and the others are on their way up?"

"No. We need to go down to check," she said.

Then she swore softly under her breath.

"Look." She pointed across the expanse at the other building.

The building's glass stairwell was filled with rebel fighters ascending toward the skyway level.

"As soon as they hit that level, they're coming across," Connor Darcy said.

"We'll hold them off while you get to the helicopter," Shepherd said, and without another word, he and Lucky sprinted for the stairwell door.

The skyway was down two flights. They raced down the stairs and were about to rush through the door when they heard a sound.

Shepherd drew up short. He leaned over and peered down the stairwell. One flight down, Pete Brody was on the ground, leaning over a man's body. He was putting his weight on the man's chest and saying something.

"Pete?" Shepherd said.

Pete looked up. He seemed dazed. They rushed down the stairs.

"Where's your family?" Lucky asked.

Pete was still leaning over the body, his palms splayed on top of the man's blood-soaked chest. It looked like he was trying to put pressure on a wound. But one quick glance and Lucky knew the man was already dead.

"What's going on, buddy?" Shepherd asked.

"Where's your family?" Lucky repeated.

He blinked and then started to stand but sank back down.

"I found him downstairs. I got him this far but then he collapsed. I can't leave him. He's ... he's..."

Lucky grabbed Pete under his armpits and hoisted him to his feet. She turned him quickly and patted him on the back.

"You did what you could. Let's go."

Pete didn't budge.

Shepherd stood in front of him. "I'm sure he was glad you were there with him when it happened. Now let's go get your wife and kids."

At the mention of his family, Pete's shock seemed to subside a bit.

"Elizabeth?"

"Yup," Lucky said. "Come on. The skyway is up one floor."

As they ran up the stairs, they saw that across the way, the rebel fighters were now only one floor below the skyway.

"Hurry!" Lucky shouted.

As they emerged onto the skyway level, the first thing Lucky saw was Elizabeth Brody with her kids on either side of her racing across the skyway. Two others were with them, a woman and an older man.

Behind them, Lucky saw a rebel fighter step into the skyway from the building's dim interior.

"Run!" Shepherd shouted.

Elizabeth turned, and when she saw the rebel fighters behind her, she grabbed her kids' hands and ran.

As she ran away from the rebel fighters, Shepherd and Lucky ran toward them, guns drawn.

Lucky saw the closest fighter lift his gun. She screamed, "Drop!"

Elizabeth Brody, her children, and the two employees hit the deck. Elizabeth was splayed on the ground, her body over her children, her arms around them.

Above them, a volley of gunfire broke out.

Elizabeth and her kids rolled to one side. The other two followed.

"Stay down!" Shepherd screamed as he ran toward the rebel fighters.

He ducked against the glass wall opposite Elizabeth, drawing fire away from them.

Lucky was behind him. When she saw a rebel fighter notice the families and turn toward them, she stepped into the middle of the skyway and shouted as she fired her gun.

With attention turned toward her, she saw the families start to army-crawl away from the other building.

"We've got to keep them distracted," she said.

"We're outnumbered and outgunned," Shepherd told her.

––––––––––––––

Above them, the sound of gunfire drew the Darcy brothers to the windows. They looked down. From an angle they could see one wall of the skyway. Both Shepherd and Lucky were pressed against it.

The glass stairwell below them was filled with rebel fighters scaling the stairs. Soon, they would also be at the skyway level.

"What are you waiting for?" Cryer screeched. "The helicopter is inbound."

"They're screwed," Connor Darcy said.

"Not our problem," his brother answered.

Then the brothers grew silent as they looked down and saw Pete Brody's family on the skyway.

"How old you think those kids are?" Connor asked.

Clint squinted out the window.

"Not old enough to drive."

"Definitely not."

"This situation, er, whatever it is, may be normal for you, but Mr. Cryer and I are a little anxious to evacuate," Lockwood said.

They ignored him.

Cryer went to stand beside them.

"I said it's time to go," he said to the brothers.

They ignored him again.

"Listen to me!" he shouted. "Are you guys professional or not? You don't want to do your jobs, is that it?"

"We're doing our job," Clint said.

"Your job is to do what I say."

"Is it?" he said.

"I paid you to protect me. You don't have a choice. Let's go."

The brothers exchanged a look.

"That's where you're wrong," Clint said.

"We always have a choice," his brother added.

A look of panic crossed Cryer's face as he saw the trail of men climbing the stairs across from them.

"I'll double what I'm paying you."

Clint laughed. "Dude, we don't do this for the money."

"Yeah, we do," his brother said.

"Well, yeah, but what I mean is that's not our main motivation."

"True."

"Are you coming or not?" Cryer said, holding the door to the roof open.

"Not," Clint said, and turned to leave.

Connor shrugged at Cryer and followed his brother back down the stairs.

Sputtering, Cryer watched them go as Lockwood pushed him into the doorway to the rooftop stairwell.

When the Darcy brothers emerged on the floor with the skyway, they found Lucky still pressed against the glass wall. Beside her, Shepherd fired at a rebel who had broken cover, darting from the dark interior of the other building as he charged onto the skyway, marching forward as he methodically fired.

As he grew closer, Lucky shouted, "He's getting too close to the families. I'm going to distract him."

She was about to step into the center of the skyway when three other rebel fighters appeared at the other side.

"There's too many of them," Shepherd said.

"We don't have a choice," she said, and stepped into the open.

At the same time, she squeezed the trigger on her weapon only to find she was out of rounds.

Panic set in when she heard a voice. "I got you."

Connor Darcy stepped in front of her and let rip a volley of rounds from his semi-automatic machine gun that instantly sent the rebels scattering.

"That's one for him," Shepherd said.

Lucky glared at him. "He's not playing."

"Oh, I'm playing all right, baby. What are we playing?"

"How about a game called convince me not to kill you for calling me baby," she said.

"I got an idea," he said, keeping his eyes glued to the scope. "Lean over and reach into the back of my pants."

"If I'm gonna cop a feel, don't you want me to buy you a drink first?" she asked.

He gave a low chuckle.

"I mean most guys have their standards. I didn't think you were easy."

Without turning his head, he answered, "I'm not like most guys, darling."

"You're right, *darling*," she said. "I have a feeling you're a much bigger pain in the ass than most."

She stepped behind him and reached for the gun that had slipped past his waistline. As she did, Shepherd happened to glance over and scowled.

Just then the rebel fighters regrouped and came out firing again.

Clint stepped forward and he and Shepherd let loose a volley of gunfire that sent the rebel fighters scuttling back to the dark interior of the worker building.

Then, Lucky had the gun out of Connor's pants. She darted to the side and crouched against the skyway's glass wall as she fired at an approaching rebel fighter opposite her. He fell with a thud a few feet from the huddled families.

A stream of fighters appeared at the skyway opening just behind the Brody family.

"Shepherd!" Lucky screamed, and pointed.

"My gun's jammed!" His head was bent and both hands were on his weapon, trying to dislodge the jam, when a rebel fighter stepped out and aimed his gun at Clint.

Lucky screamed, "Watch out!"

Clint looked up as the sound of gunfire and breaking glass erupted into the air.

The rebel fighter fell to the ground. The glass wall beside him had a neat set of cracks where a bullet had entered.

Clint let out a whoop. "Wow. Saw my life flash before my eyes on that one."

Shepherd looked at Lucky.

She shrugged. "For once it wasn't me."

"Me neither," he said, and frowned.

Connor Darcy shrugged. "Wasn't me."

They all turned to look outside. But the only thing in the direction the bullet came from was a water silo on top of the factory building.

"If we didn't shoot him, who did?" Lucky asked Shepherd.

"Beats me." He turned to Clint. "You're one lucky son of a gun."

Clint grinned. "Aw, that's no big thing. Just my guardian angel."

Lucky frowned, and he winked at her.

For a few seconds, the other side of the skyway was silent and still. Lucky saw a few bodies pressed against the glass wall near the interior entryway. They were too close to the families. She didn't like it. She was about to step forward and fire to drive them even further back inside when she saw something that made her blood turn cold.

The rebel fighters had turned to run. As they did, one looked out the window down at the ground.

Pete Brody was suddenly beside her, also looking down. Then he turned and screamed at his family, "Run!"

Elizabeth scrambled to her feet, pulling her kids with her as they ran toward Pete.

Lucky raced to the window—below her a truck skidded to a stop underneath the skyway. A split second later, an RPG was launched from its bed, squealing into the air.

A massive explosion rocked the floor underneath her as the rocket hit the skyway.

The air was filled with a fireball, black smoke, the tinkle of shattering glass, and then, with a tremendous groan of bending metal, the skyway began to collapse.

25

As soon as the dust settled, all was quiet.

There was a pile of rubble near the center of the bridge and no movement.

Pete Brody ran toward the skyway's collapsing center but only got a few feet before Shepherd grabbed him and held him back.

"You're an engineer. How long is that thing going to hold?"

Pete shook his head wildly and strained against Shepherd's hold. "Liz? Cassidy? Will?" he shouted.

Behind them, Clint Darcy was swearing.

Lucky turned and saw that his brother was on the ground. He'd been shot. Clint was kneeling down and putting pressure on a wound gushing blood. Within seconds, Lucky was beside him, ripping off a strip of her T-shirt and offering it to help create a tourniquet.

Clint looked up gratefully.

Lucky met his eyes. "We need to get him to the helicopter. I'll help."

"Nah," Connor said weakly, and winked. "This is just a flesh wound. Like a mosquito bite. It's nothing."

But his face was clearly furrowed in pain.

"Listen to the lady, brother," Clint said.

Behind them Pete was still screaming his wife's name in desperation.

Then he shouted, "Thank God. Come on, baby, let's get you across."

Lucky and the two brothers looked over and saw Elizabeth emerging from the rubble as the smoke cleared, her children·beside her. She leaned down and checked two bodies lying nearby. Sadly, she shook her head.

"Shepherd," Lucky said. "We need to get Connor to the helicopter. Right now."

Her voice was low but urgent.

"What about my family?" Pete demanded.

With his brother's help, Connor pulled himself upright.

"Let's get the kids first," he said, and looked at Lucky. "What? Maybe I'm not such a big pain in the ass after all?"

She hid her smile and looked away.

"Let's get the family and get the hell out of here."

"The bridge is about to collapse," Lucky said.

"I can get them across before it does, but I need to hurry," Pete said.

"You sure?" Shepherd asked.

"I'm going to have to be." His voice was fierce. "You just keep them from shooting my family while I'm doing this."

"We got it," Clint said.

Following Pete, they all made their way toward the collapsing center of the bridge.

At one point, Shepherd raised his gun and fired.

A rebel fighter who had emerged from the building's dim interior fell dead.

Elizabeth visibly shivered but did not turn around. Her kids screamed. She put her arms around them and said something to calm them.

Another fighter popped out, and this time, Clint and Connor took him out with two shots.

Pete, who was leading the way, held up his palm.

"This is far enough for you guys. I don't think we should put too much weight on it."

Everyone except Pete stopped and he kept going, walking carefully.

Soon he was close to the center, where a long, thick strip of rebar held the bridge together.

Elizabeth and the kids were on the other side, about ten feet away.

"Daddy, I'm scared," Will said.

"I know, sport. It's okay," he said. "I'm going to get you across."

Cassidy looked down at the hole in the skyway and the ground far below before quickly glancing away.

"This is about as close as I can get," Pete said. "Elizabeth, you and the kids weigh less, but I'm still going to have you cross one at a time just to be safe. I'll walk you through it. Just put one foot in front of the other."

Elizabeth nodded.

"I can't." Will looked at the rebar. "I'll fall."

"You won't," Pete said. "Just pretend that you're walking along that small wall on the way to school. Remember how you used to do that every day? You never fell off that wall and it was even more narrow than this bar."

"Yeah, but if I fell it was only a foot or something."

"But you never fell, did you, buddy?"

Will shook his head.

Elizabeth walked him to the edge of the bridge.

She knelt beside him. "You can do this. I know you can."

"Mom, I can't. What if I trip? Or miss my step?"

Tears streamed down his face.

"You won't," she said. "You have great balance, remember?"

"He can't, Dad," Cassidy wailed. "You can't make us do this. Can't we just go downstairs and come up the elevator to your side?"

Seconds later, Lucky lifted her gun and picked off another rebel fighter behind them.

"Listen!" Pete shouted, pointing up. "That sound is the helicopter landing. It's not going to wait long for us. We need to be on that helicopter. I need you to walk across now."

"No!" Will crossed his arms.

At that moment, they heard a tremendous rending sound of metal before the strip of rebar shifted and then broke, dropping several feet below the skyway, where it hung vertically.

Without a word, Elizabeth scooped Will into her arms and then met Pete's eyes.

He nodded.

Turning to the side to get momentum, Elizabeth gave a loud grunt and tossed her son across the void. He screamed as he flew through the air.

Pete braced his feet along a bent piece of the sloped skyway floor and reached toward Will's airborne body.

Just missing his dad's outstretched arms, Will landed hard on the skyway floor. But then he immediately began to slide down the sloped surface. He screamed again and scrambled to grab ahold of something on the crumbling bridge floor.

Pete lunged forward and grabbed Will's hands as the boy slid toward the abyss. Now Pete was lying down, holding onto his son's hands. He was nearly vertical, his toes gripping the flatter surface above. His son's body was angling off the edge of the sloped surface from the waist down.

"Hold on, son."

"I can't, Dad. It's too hard," Will said.

"Just ten more seconds."

Pete Brody inched forward to try to tighten his grip. He started to slip.

"Grab his ankles!" Clint Darcy said.

"No!" Lucky shouted. "It will be too much weight."

"I can't hold on anymore," the boy said.

Pete reached down and grabbed Will by the wrists right before the boy's grip slipped. Then he quickly pulled the boy to his chest and scrambled backward up to the flat surface of the skyway. When he reached it, he hauled Will away from the edge.

Seconds later, another chunk of the bridge fell.

There was no longer a sloped surface, just the two jagged edges of the skyway. The side Pete stood on was about three feet lower than the side his wife and daughter were on.

Elizabeth and Pete stared at each other across the abyss.

"You and Will need to get on that helicopter," she said.

"You and Cassidy can make the jump," Pete said. "It would have been too hard for Will but you both have long legs. Get a running start. You can do it. I know you can."

"Daddy!" Cassidy was crying hysterically. "You know I can't. I'm too scared. You know how I am about heights. Please, Daddy. Come and get me. I can't jump. I just can't."

"You can do it, champ," he said.

"I can't. I swear. Please don't leave us here."

"I'm not going without you," he said.

"You are," Elizabeth said.

"No, I'm not."

Just then the sound of a helicopter drew everyone's eyes up to the sky.

"Go!" Liz said.

"Jump," Pete said. "You can do it."

"It's too dangerous," Elizabeth said. "I'm staying with her."

"What?" Cassidy said. "No! We have to go with Dad."

"Then you need to jump," Elizabeth said calmly.

"I can't. You know why."

Liz leaned down and said something to her daughter. The girl looked up and nodded.

"We'll meet you at the helicopter," Elizabeth said.

Pete nodded grimly.

Then, without a word, Elizabeth grabbed her daughter's hand. They both turned and began walking toward the building without looking back.

Pete stood and watched them with silent tears streaming down his face.

26

As soon as Lockwood and Cryer entered the glass stairwell, they heard shouting and heavy footsteps.

Lockwood leaned over and looked down.

Rebel fighters were running up the stairs below them.

He reached into his jacket and took out a pistol.

Cryer blinked. "You have a gun?"

Without answering, Lockwood leaned over and fired down.

After he fired a few shots, Lockwood turned to Cryer. "Let's go."

"You killed someone?" Cryer's eyes widened.

"Him or us."

A second later, bullets shattered the railing near Cryer. He swore loudly.

"Go!" Lockwood said. "Hurry."

As Cryer ran up the stairs, he said in a frantic voice, "I don't want to die, Lockwood."

"Run!" Lockwood said.

Within seconds they were right below the small staircase leading to the rooftop helipad.

More shouting from below.

Lockwood leaned over the edge and quickly surveyed the scene before ducking just as a bullet whipped past him.

"There's three of them," he said, reloading his gun. "I think I can take them."

"What about the helicopter?"

"It's not leaving without you," Lockwood said. "But if we don't get rid of these guys, they are coming up on the helipad and maybe taking out the pilot before we can even board."

Cryer was silent for a second as that registered.

"Get me out of here alive and a million dollars of that money is yours," he shouted over his shoulder.

Lockwood didn't answer. Instead, he leaned over and fired methodically for a few seconds.

"Done."

"Thank God."

"A million, huh?" he said to Cryer.

Cryer nodded.

"I know you have a lot more than a million in this duffel bag," he said. "And in your bag? How much is that diamond worth anyway?"

But Cryer was looking out a window at the courtyard below the two buildings.

When Cryer didn't answer, Lockwood looked down as well.

Tiberius stood on the ground looking up at them. He was flanked by two massive wolves who stood with their heads close to his thighs.

Behind him stood a man with longer hair. At one point, the wolves looked back at the man.

A smirk spread across Cryer's face.

"He's lost. He thought he could intimidate me, but he's lost."

In a show of defiance, Cryer held up the small bag containing the diamond. Then he ordered Lockwood to hand him the duffel bag. Leaning over, he waved the duffle bag so Tiberius could see it.

The rebel warlord remained expressionless.

Even from a distance, Cryer could see the man's lips move as he kept his eyes on the two men in the glass stairwell landing.

Then he gave a slight nod and a car pulled up beside him.

Two rebel fighters opened the door and dragged a man out of the backseat.

It was Drake Martin. His clothes were torn and he was covered in blood. The men shoved him to the ground in front of Tiberius.

Tiberius kept his eyes trained on Cryer.

The two fighters drew their guns and shot Drake.

His body jerked from the impact and then lay still.

Keeping his eyes aloft, Tiberius never took his gaze off Cryer.

27

Pete Brody stood there staring at his wife and daughter as they walked away until they disappeared into the building.

Lucky trailed behind the others heading toward the helicopter.

At the end of the skyway, she turned.

"Mr. Brody?" she said. "We have to go now."

Pete started to turn and then there was a loud sound. He rushed to the glass wall and looked down.

Another convoy of fighters had just pulled into the compound. They were unloading a sea of armed men who were filing into the lobby of the workers' building.

The building Liz and Cassidy were in.

He ran to the edge of the bridge and began to scream.

"Liz!" he shouted, and then he remembered.

Putting his fingers to his lips, he let out an ear-splitting whistle like he used to do when he called the kids home for lunch during those long summer days.

He waited.

Seconds later, Liz appeared with Cassidy.

"Liz!" he shouted. "Look!"

She followed where his finger was pointing and then walked over to the edge of the window holding her daughter's hand.

When Cassidy saw what he was pointing out, she burst into tears.

"They're coming up the stairs," he shouted.

Elizabeth and Cassidy ran back to the edge of the skyway.

"You have to jump, sweetie," Pete said to his daughter. "Just close your eyes and jump."

"I can't, Daddy. I can't do it."

"Let's do it together," Liz said.

She grabbed her daughter's hand and pulled her as they backed up. "We'll get a running start and hold hands and do it together."

Tears were pouring down Cassidy's face. "I can't, Mom. I'm scared."

"I know, honey. I know you are, but you can do this. I know you can."

"I can't."

"Remember that time you had to sing that solo during the Christmas concert?" Liz asked. "You said you could never sing in front of that many people but you decided to overcome your fears and try it. And you killed it. You got a standing ovation. And you were so proud of yourself after. This is going to be like that."

Gunfire echoed within the building behind them.

Cassidy jumped and burst into fresh tears.

"Do you think you can try for me?"

Cassidy gave an alarmed look behind them at the sound of more gunshots and nodded.

"Okay," Liz said. "On the count of three, we're going to run and jump. Just like when you were in track and did the long jump. You were always good at that event, remember? Think of it just like that."

"I wasn't good. I never placed."

"But you still jumped a long way, right?"

Cassidy gave a morose nod.

There was a loud sound behind them. Liz cast a nervous glance over her shoulder.

"We're going to do it just like that. On the count of three."

"Keep your eyes on me!" Pete said. He stood at the other edge with his arms stretched out over the gap. "Right here, champ. Just keep watching me."

"One! Two! Three!" Liz shouted.

Then they were running toward the void, Cassidy with a look of sheer terror on her face. They were almost to the edge when Cassidy looked down. She balked. Not a lot, but enough.

But they were already launched in the air. Liz, who had a death grip on her daughter's left hand, whipped her own right arm forward as they flew through the air, and the extra momentum propelled Cassidy forward enough for her to land in her father's arms just as Liz let go of her hand.

Pete Brody grasped his daughter in his arms and then pivoted to fling her onto the ground behind him.

"Run!" he shouted. She scrambled to her feet and ran toward Lucky, who had her arms outstretched.

He turned back around.

Liz had landed in a crouched position on the jagged remaining edge of the skyway, but when she tried to stand, a piece under her right foot broke off.

Suddenly there was nothing but air beneath her foot and she teetered, losing her balance. Her eyes grew wide and she reached forward into the empty space as her body began to sway backward.

Pete lunged forward and managed to grasp her wrist and yank her to safety. They fell backward onto the floor just as another chunk broke free.

Then they were on their feet, sprinting toward the building.

"We need to run to make the helicopter," Lucky said.

"I think some of the rebel fighters are on the floor above," Clint Darcy said.

Lucky patted her gun. "We'll handle them."

Connor Darcy was leaning against the wall, breathing heavily, his face drained of color.

"You're not looking too good," Shepherd said.

Blood was oozing out of his wound.

"We need a proper bandage and better tourniquet," Lucky said.

Connor tried to take a step but nearly tipped over.

Shepherd grabbed his arm to steady him.

"Why don't you let me carry you up to the roof?" he offered.

Clint stepped forward and nodded. "Much appreciated, but brothers carry their brothers to the end."

Shepherd gave a respectful nod and took a step backward. "Then let us clear the path for you."

28

Lucky flung open the door to the next floor and then stood back.

When nothing happened, she poked her head around the corner.

"Clear," she said in a low voice.

She and Shepherd charged up the stairwell. When they got to the next landing, Shepherd hung his head over the edge.

"Clear. Come on up."

"Go!" It was Clint Darcy, urging Pete Brody and his family forward. They ran up the stairs. Then, with his brother flung over his shoulder, Clint followed them.

As soon as the group was huddled on the landing, Lucky had them all stand back as she cracked the door. She held out three fingers to indicate three rebel fighters standing near the door to the roof.

Lucky started to count down, dropping her fingers one by one.

By the time she had a closed fist, she and Shepherd kicked open the door and opened fire. They managed to take out two of the fighters, but a third took cover behind a pillar. He continued to fire as Lucky and Shepherd charged into the hallway.

Lucky ducked behind another pillar and then dropped and scrambled until she had a view of the man's leg. She aimed and fired, hitting him in the upper thigh.

He yowled in pain but turned toward Lucky, pointing a pistol her way. Then Shepherd was on him and took him out with one clean shot to the head.

"That's one," he said in a low voice, and then bellowed louder, "Let's go!"

The Darcy brothers and the Brody family poured out of the doorway.

"This way," Lucky said, opening the stairwell door leading to the roof.

As the door opened, the sound of the helicopter nearly drowned out her words.

She motioned for the others to go first.

Shepherd led with his assault rifle, taking the stairs two at a time. When he got to the landing, he waited for the others.

Pete Brody picked up Will and ran up the stairs with Cassidy, Liz right behind him. Their faces were red and tear-streaked.

As they passed, Lucky gave a grim smile. "You got this. We're almost there."

Then Clint Darcy walked in with his brother over his shoulder, grimacing with the effort.

"Why don't we both carry him," Lucky said.

"Thanks," Clint said gruffly, "but I'm good. You just cover my back. I heard some noises in the hall behind me."

"Noted."

As he grunted up the stairwell, he said, "Never thought I'd ask a woman to cover my six."

"First time for everything, cowboy," Lucky said.

He chuckled.

His brother, slung over his shoulder, was moaning now. His eyes were closed.

Lucky swallowed a lump of dread.

"Let's go. We need medics asap," she said.

She tried her wrist comm again.

"Red, if you can read me, we're sending civilians on board the helicopter. They're going to need medics asap when they land. Shepherd and I are going to stay behind and find Mako. We'll update you when she's located."

"You're staying behind?" Clint said over his shoulder.

"Our protectee is missing," Lucky said.

"Well, we've abandoned ours," he said. "You got to realize there comes a time when it's every man for himself, sweetheart."

"You didn't think that earlier. You and your brother stayed behind to help that family."

"That was different."

Lucky nodded. "I get it. But the difference is your protectee deserved to be abandoned. Mine doesn't deserve that."

"Fair enough."

Shepherd threw open the door, and after making sure no rebel fighters had infiltrated the roof, he began to shout and wave the Brody family through. "Go! Go! Go!" he said.

"Run!" Lucky screamed, and stepped out the door behind the Darcy brothers.

"Of course Cryer is already here. He better make room," she said, watching as Cryer and Lockwood climbed into the helicopter. The pilot had turned the engine off. When he saw them, he restarted it.

"Let's go," she said. "They're not leaving without you guys."

When she turned, she saw Shepherd at the edge of the roof, looking down.

"Shepherd?" Lucky called. He held up a hand behind him.

Curious, she ran over to the edge and peered down.

"Oh, shit," she said.

Clint Darcy paused when he heard it. He did a half turn and poked his head over the roof.

Tiberius stood on the ground below, lit up by the compound's orange lights. A massive armored truck was beside him, its back roof unfolding like the top of a convertible.

Tiberius stood staring up at them, his two wolves at his side.

"What is that?" Shepherd said. "What is he getting ready to do?"

"I'm afraid to find out," Clint Darcy said.

"He looks really confident, and that scares me," Lucky said.

Shepherd let out a low whistle. "This can't be good."

Lucky turned toward the Darcy brothers. "Right now would be a really good time for your guardian angel to show up again."

29

"Run!" Shepherd shouted.

Everyone bolted for the helicopter.

The rotor blades were picking up speed again.

"Wait!" Lucky shouted when she realized that Clint was struggling to run with his brother over his shoulder.

They were about ten feet away when Lockwood appeared in the helicopter doorway, holding a gun. The gun wobbled crazily as his arms shook.

"Stay back!" he shouted.

Lucky, who was closest to him, took a step back and put her hands in the air, palms facing him.

Neither she nor Shepherd had a chance to draw their weapons.

Lockwood had them pinned.

"Don't reach for your guns or I'll kill you. I did it already today. I killed someone."

"Easy now," she said. "There's no need for that gun. We're all on the same side here. There's plenty of room. These bad boys hold more weight than you'd think."

"No!" he shouted. "It's just for us."

Lucky shouted over her shoulder.

"Brody! Stairs! Now!"

Shepherd and Clint Darcy formed a human wall as the Brody family backed up toward the stairwell.

Once the door closed on them, Shepherd stepped forward and Lockwood swiveled, pointing the gun at the larger man's chest. "Back off! I'm serious. I'll shoot you. I shot people already. I killed people!"

His voice rose to a level of hysteria with the last few words. Sweat was pouring down his brow despite the frigid air and his eyes were darting from one person to the other.

"Yes, you said that," Lucky said in a calm voice. "You killed the enemy. Good job. But we're not the enemy. We're on your side."

"Let us onboard. Now," Clint demanded.

"You just want the money and the diamond."

"The diamond?" Shepherd said. "You're crazy, man. We just want to get out of here alive. Same as you."

Lockwood's hands were still shaking madly. He moved his finger toward the gun's trigger.

"I don't believe you. You're going to take it all away from us. That's why you're here in the first place."

"Not true," Lucky said.

Clint spoke quickly.

"Easy now," he said as he moved to set his brother down. "I'm just going to set him down for a second. You know that's not true. You hired us to protect you. Now let us do our job."

Lockwood's frenzied gaze turned to his hired bodyguard team.

"He's dead. Your brother is dead. He can't even protect himself. You can't even protect your own brother."

At Lockwood's words, Clint looked down and saw his brother on the ground, eyes wide in a vacant stare.

Lucky saw what was happening a second too late. She reached to grab Clint's forearm to stop him but he was already charging Lockwood with a strangled scream.

"No!" she shouted.

But Lockwood pivoted and fired.

Clint dropped to the rooftop in a crumpled heap.

Both Lucky and Shepherd drew their guns and charged Lockwood.

He turned the gun toward Shepherd, who was in front.

Right before Lockwood's finger squeezed the trigger, a shot rang out.

At that moment, the helicopter lifted into the air and Lockwood tumbled out of the open doorway onto the roof, a bullet hole in the center of his forehead.

Lucky and Shepherd looked around, searching for the sniper.

She saw a glint of something on the factory building's water silo.

A tremendous boom filled the air. The compound went dark.

"EMP!" Shepherd shouted. He was leaning over the edge of the roof, looking down at where Tiberius had been. "The electronics are shot."

The helicopter, now up in the air, spun wildly out of control. It twisted sideways and then hurtled downward, ricocheting and slicing into one wall of the factory before smashing into the ground with a massive explosion and fireball.

Standing at the edge of the roof looking down, Lucky squinted. "What the hell is all that stuff floating in the air? It looks like little pieces of paper on fire."

Shepherd reached for his binoculars. He lifted them to his eyes and said, "Cold. Hard. Cash. About three million dollars' worth. Burning up."

The pieces of the exploded helicopter were spread out across the empty ground below.

"Bet that diamond that Lockwood was so worried about didn't burn," Lucky said.

"That might be the only thing that survives this night," Shepherd said in a low voice.

Lucky wiped sweat off her brow and turned to see the Brody family peeking through the stairwell door.

"It's clear," she said, and waved them over.

"Was that the helicopter?" Pete asked.

"Tiberius detonated an EMP bomb. Took out the electronics every-where, including in the chopper," Shepherd said.

Lucky, who was still leaning over the roof, shook her head.

"We're sitting ducks up here, Shepherd," she said.

"We need to get to that access gate in the back," he said.

Pete Brody joined Shepherd at the edge to see where he was pointing.

"There's no way out of this building," Lucky said. "The fighters just keep coming in the front gate."

He and Lucky exchanged a look.

"Here." Shepherd swooped down and grabbed the gun Lockwood had in his hands, a .50-caliber assault rifle. He silently handed it to Pete, who took it and nodded.

Then Shepherd reached into an ankle holster and withdrew a tiny pistol.

"This one's easy. Just point and squeeze here," he said, handing it to Elizabeth Brody. She took it and gave a grim nod.

"I can shoot," Will said. "Give me one."

"Sorry, buddy. You might be a dead eye, but I'm not giving you a gun. Not right now, at least," Shepherd said.

Elizabeth, who had been peering over the edge at the stairwell, stepped forward.

"You're both putting on a brave face and I appreciate that, but you know and I know we don't have enough bullets or guns to stop what's coming," she said. "Is there any place to hide or protect our kids until this is over?"

Everyone looked at each other solemnly.

"If I know they will survive," she said, "that's all I need to know. That's enough."

30

As the small group stood looking at each other and the stairwell door, a loud grunt came from the other side of the helipad.

Heads swiveled.

Lucky opened her mouth in astonishment.

A man stood next to the small wall at the edge of the building.

He was identical to the two Darcy brothers, who lay dead a few feet away.

"There's three of them," Will said.

"It's called triplets, dummy," his sister said.

The man ignored the group gathered by the stairwell and walked toward the bodies of his two brothers.

Then he was on the ground, pulling both of his brothers close. Tenderly, he lifted first Clint's head and then Connor's and rested them in his lap. He leaned over them, speaking to them in a low voice.

"Where the hell did he come from?" Lucky squinted suspiciously at the brother.

"He must have climbed the wall of the building," Shepherd whispered.

They walked over to where the man had popped up and peered

over the edge, where an emergency rope ladder hung down to the ground. They turned back to watch the brother.

After a few seconds of speaking to his dead brothers, he took his thumb and pressed it into a pool of blood on the roof. Slowly, still speaking words Lucky couldn't make out, he made the sign of the cross on Clint's forehead. Removing his thumb, he leaned down, kissed his brother's cheek, and then slipped a chain with dog tags off Clint's neck. He looped the chain around his own neck, then set his brother's body gently to the side. Then he dipped his thumb into the blood again and did the same thing with Connor's body.

When he looked up and stared into the distance, his eyes were glazed.

He pulled himself to his feet and plodded over to Shepherd and Lucky, dipping his head in greeting.

"You're the sniper who saved my butt down there," Shepherd said. "Thank you. I owe you."

"You had my brothers' back. I saw it. We're more than even."

"You're their guardian angel," Lucky said in a soft voice.

The brother raised his eyes to meet hers and shook his head. "Fallen angel, maybe. I couldn't save them. Not this time."

"I'm so sorry," Lucky said. "They were good men."

"She's right," Shepherd said. "I don't say that about just anyone. They were stand-up guys."

"I'm Colton. Colton Darcy."

After introductions were made, Lucky said, "You were your brothers' secret weapon. Does anybody even know you exist?"

He gave a grim smile. "Nah. This is why the Darcy brothers are legends—surviving the unsurvivable. Nobody ever knew we were three. But all that's over now."

Shepherd said, "I have a feeling a lot is going to be over now."

Lucky shot a look at the Brody family huddled near the door.

Shepherd headed toward the edge of the roof to look down.

"Think we could get everyone down that ladder you used?" Lucky asked Colton.

"It would be slow going," he said, and glanced over at the group by the stairwell. "But probably. If we can secure the kids."

"We're surrounded," Shepherd said as he walked back over. "This rebel warlord seems to have an endless supply of fighters. They just keep coming."

"We better get started going down that ladder, then," Lucky said.

"And then what?" Shepherd squinted over the side of the building. "They're guarding the back access door and the front gate."

Pete Brody stepped forward and gave a grim smile.

"If you don't mind," he began. "I have a plan."

"What?" Lucky said suspiciously.

"Hold this." Pete handed her the .50-caliber assault rifle. "Get us to the ground and I know a way out."

"We can't leave without Mako," she said. "When was the last time you saw her?"

"In the offices."

Shepherd started toward the stairwell door. "I'll go get her," he said. "Lucky, you lead them out of here."

Just then a small door on the opposite side of the helipad opened and Mako crawled out. Her pencil skirt was ripped, her hair tangled, and her face streaked with dirt.

"Oh good, you're still here," she said. "I was locked in the vault and then all the lights went out and the door opened."

"Tiberius detonated an EMP," Shepherd said.

She nodded. "I heard them in the hall so I climbed into the ventilation system because I knew I could access the roof. But I heard them in the room underneath. They were in the office. I think they were looking for the cash and the diamond."

"Makes sense," Shepherd said.

"It won't take them long to search and realize nothing is there. They're on their way to the roof. They said that would be the next stop."

"Who's this?" Colton finally asked.

"We met already," she said in a prim voice.

"Nah, you met my brothers." He pointed to the two bodies.

Mako blanched and gave a visible shiver.

"Here," Elizabeth Brody said, and pulled a lightweight down jacket out of her backpack.

"Thanks," Mako said.

Colton walked over to a series of pipes and broke off a thin metal one.

"She said they're coming up the stairs. We've got to brace this door. We're going to need some time to get down that ladder."

"Let's go!" Shepherd shouted, and gestured for the Brody family to follow as he and Lucky headed for the edge of the roof.

"Start down that ladder," Lucky said. "I'll be right behind you."

She rummaged in her small backpack.

"I've been saving this," she said, withdrawing a small detonation device. "I think now is the right time."

"What's that, darling?" Colton asked.

Lucky frowned at the name but continued to stick the wires to the edges of the door.

"Just a little diversion that should buy us some time."

Securing the explosive, she zipped up her backpack and headed toward the other side of the helipad.

"I'm not going down that," Cassidy was saying to Pete Brody. "I can't, Dad. I can't."

He crouched before her and took her hands. "You can. You leaped across that," he said, pointing to the nearly collapsed skyway.

"I can't even look over there."

"This is going to be easier," he said. "You don't look down. I'm going to go first so I'll be right below you. You just concentrate on my voice. I'll walk you through every step. It's just like that old ladder to the tree fort at Grandpa's farm, remember?"

"I hated that tree fort and those stairs," she said.

"Listen," Pete said in a low voice. "You are stronger than your brother. It's going to be more challenging for him to get down. Your legs are longer and your grip is better. I'm asking you something now that I wouldn't normally ask. I need you to be brave for him and show that you're not afraid."

She shot a glance at her brother, who was watching the others barricade the door to the stairs.

"Can you do that for me?" Pete asked.

"Yes." She nodded.

"We're going over," he said, and stood. "I'll go first. Then Cassidy, then Liz, and then Will."

"I'll be next," Lucky said.

"We're ready to rock and roll," Colton said, surveying the barricade. "This will hold them for a while. Let's go now."

Pete stood at the edge of the building, his legs already on the first few rungs of the ladder.

"Dad?" Will asked.

Cassidy crouched in front of him like her father had just done with her. She took his hands in hers.

"You got this, Will," she said. "Just like going down from Grandpa's tree fort."

She looked at her father and winked.

Will gulped and nodded. Then Pete Brody went down, followed by the rest of his family. Lucky was about to step onto the ladder when someone banged on the door.

"Let's go, let's go, let's go!" Colton Darcy said.

He followed Lucky, with Shepherd behind him.

Shepherd was over the wall with his feet on the rungs when he heard a shout. He ducked his head below the wall right as an explosion rocked the rooftop as the door and stairwell blew up.

31

The wolf handler stood back and watched Tiberius lose his cool.

Once again.

The biggest mistake the wolf handler ever made was turning over his beloved wolves to this violent, impetuous toddler.

Tiberius was screaming. His face was bright red.

"The diamond. The money. Go!" He pointed to a plume of black smoke above the roof of the plastics factory. "Find that satchel Cryer was holding."

He stood back and arched his neck to try to see the rooftop where the helipad was located.

"What is taking them so long?" He shook his radio. "They were trapped on the roof. Why haven't we heard back from the advance team?"

He turned to the man beside him, who shrugged.

The wolf handler, still listening, narrowed his eyes.

The longer he was around Tiberius, the more he felt like he was watching a puppet, a man pretending to be a warlord.

"Status?" Tiberius was shouting into his radio.

"We're breaching the roof door now."

A second later, they heard an explosion.

Tiberius looked up and saw flames and smoke from the rooftop.

"Status?" he shouted again.

There was only static.

Tiberius walked around the side of the building to see the crash scene without the factory building obstructing the view.

The handler followed. The wolves looked back at him once, and when he didn't make a signal, they continued loping alongside Tiberius. The handler followed but stayed a ways back.

Tiberius was staring off at the horizon when suddenly his head jerked to the side.

The handler followed his gaze.

There was motion along the side of the tall building.

People were crawling down a ladder.

"Get them!" Tiberius shouted, his arm stretched out, his finger pointing. "Now!"

The man he yelled at balked.

"Our men are going after the diamond," the man finally said.

"Send someone else!"

"We don't have anyone else."

"How many men do we still have?" Tiberius asked.

"Seven, sir."

"Impossible!"

32

As soon as his feet hit the ground, Shepherd turned to Pete.

"Where to, boss? It's time for that plan of yours."

"The factory," Pete said, his lips pressed together with determination.

Lucky and Colton crept to the edge of the building and poked their heads around. To get to the factory door, they had to cross the empty space between the CEO building and the workers' building, putting them right in the line of fire.

"Half a dozen fighters heading our way," Lucky said, and ducked back just as a volley of gunfire erupted.

"I'll hold them off while you make a break for the other side." Colton lifted his assault rifle.

"I'm not going," Cassidy said. "I can't. It's too much. I'm done running. I'm done fighting."

Pete leaned down. "Here's the deal, honey," he said. "When they say run, I want you to run as fast as you can. I'll be holding your hand. We're going to get to that door." He pointed. "See it?"

Cassidy nodded.

"That door is leading us to a secret tunnel that will get us out of here. Do you trust me?"

She looked at her father for a few seconds and then nodded.

Pete turned to Lucky.

"There's a tunnel inside. It was supposed to stream clean water to a nearby village. It will take us there."

"We'll lay down suppressive fire," Colton said.

"On three, I need you to run as fast as you can," Lucky said.

Pete began to pick up Will but the boy pushed him away.

"I'll slow you down, Dad," he said, pulling his shoulders back. "I can run fast, remember?"

"Yes, son, I remember."

The family crouched at the corner of the building, ready to run, with Mako next to them.

"Get ready," Lucky said. "Try to run in a line that gives them less of a target."

"Dad!" Cassidy said.

Before anyone could answer, Lucky began the countdown.

"One...two...three...go! Now!" she shouted.

The Brody family and Mako raced toward the shelter of the factory wall as Colton, Lucky, and Shepherd stepped out from behind the building and let loose a flurry of gunfire.

Shepherd looked over at the Brody family. They were standing in front of the factory door, which was still closed. He frowned.

Pete was tugging at the door and then working on the keypad.

"Something's wrong," Shepherd said.

"The EMP," Colton said. "It took the door's electronics down, too."

"This isn't good," Lucky said. "I'm going to hang back and cover you if needed. Then you can cover me when I go across."

Shepherd nodded. "Good plan. Let's go!"

He and Colton darted out and raced across the gap, firing as they did.

When they were halfway across the open space, a man stepped out behind a vehicle with a rocket launcher. He lifted it toward Shepherd and Colton.

Lucky stepped out from behind the building and let out a bloodcurdling scream. When the man turned toward her, she let loose a volley from the .50-caliber assault rifle.

By then Colton and Shepherd had reached the other side and stepped out to provide suppressive fire while she made her own mad dash.

As soon as she ducked behind the building, she gave Shepherd a high five and said, slightly out of breath, "One for me."

"What's all that about?" Colton asked.

"Long story." Shepherd shook his head.

Once everyone was gathered in front of the factory door, Lucky and Colton kept their backs to the family and their guns raised, looking for any approaching fighters.

Mako and Pete Brody were frantically trying their keycards on the keypad.

Nothing was happening.

Cassidy was panicking.

Lucky and Colton fired a few shots toward the back of the building.

"They're going to kill us," Cassidy said. "They're coming!"

"Dad!" Will said. "You said all I had to do was run over here. You lied!"

"Will!" Liz Brody said. "That's enough!"

The boy tugged on Shepherd's hand. "Help us! Tell us what to do!"

Shepherd looked over at Pete for a second before he spoke.

"Let me think," Pete said.

"Your dad is going to get us out of here," Shepherd said. "I'm not worried. Let's give him time to think. A moment of quiet, please!"

Pete turned to Lucky and Colton.

"Can you cover me for a second?" he asked, then began making his way to the side of the building.

"No!" Cassidy screamed.

Pete ducked back around and nodded.

"What's the move?" Shepherd said.

"The helicopter took out part of the plant wall when it crashed. We can access the factory—and the tunnel—that way."

Liz turned to her kids. "We're going to follow your dad. Cassidy, you first. Will next. I'll follow. Don't turn around. Don't look back."

The Brody family lined up near the edge of the building. Mako fell in line behind them.

"On my count," Shepherd said. He looked at Lucky and Colton.

"We've got a few rounds left," she said.

Shepherd walked over to them and then said over his shoulder, "One ... two ... three ...Go!"

With suppressive gunfire erupting behind them, the Brody family began their mad dash for the factory wall.

After they rounded the corner, Liz blanched, stopping for half a second before shouting, "Just keep your eyes on your father!"

Large chunks of the helicopters were still on fire and its debris was spread out over the area. Two blackened, charred bodies lay off to the side. Remnants of partially burned cash was scattered across the snow. A few small pockets of debris were still aflame like mini bonfires.

"Don't look!" Pete shouted over his shoulder as he ran.

They were almost to the hole in the factory wall when Will dipped down and scooped something up so fast only Cassidy noticed.

"What was that?" she asked.

"You'll see." He glanced behind him and saw that two fighters had seen him from a distance. One was pointing at him. He turned and ran.

Mako nearly ran into Elizabeth, who stopped quickly to avoid running into her son.

"Will! Go! I said no stopping, no turning around!" Liz's voice was frantic.

Pete swore loudly as he got to the hole in the factory wall.

A large burning piece of the helicopter lay in the gaping hole, flames licking up from it, blocking the way.

Pete looked around quickly and saw a large piece of metal.

As his family caught up to him, he stuck the end of the pole under the burning hunk of metal with a loud grunt and lifted it up and over to one side.

Dropping the metal pole, he tossed Will through the opening before pushing Cassidy and Liz in behind him.

Seconds later, Mako, Lucky, Shepherd, and Colton Darcy followed.

"Here!" Pete shouted. "Over here! Follow my voice."

A very dim light came in from the hole in the wall. They ran toward Pete's voice. He was stopped in front of an open door.

There was a deep blackness inside.

A damp, putrid smell wafted out.

"P.U.," Will said.

As they stood in the silence, small animal noises—squeaking and skittering—and the rhythmic patter of dripping water echoed out of the tunnel.

"What are those noises?" Cassidy said.

"Maybe baby mice," Elizabeth said. "Remember those baby mice your cousin Melissa had at her farm and how cute they were?"

"Yeah," she said. "Are you sure?"

Elizabeth didn't answer.

Pete cleared his throat. "The tunnel runs about a mile and then we'll surface at the village."

"You go first, honey," Elizabeth said. "We'll do the same order. Cassidy and then Will. I'll bring up the back."

The family dipped inside.

The sound of shouting from outside the building seemed to be growing closer.

"Pete," Shepherd said. "If you can, run. Don't wait for us in case we need to hold them off."

"Okay. We'll meet you in the village."

The sound of their footsteps echoed.

"You're next, Lucky," Shepherd said. " I want you right behind them in case there's an ambush on the other side. Maybe stop them and go out the tunnel first."

"Roger that," Lucky said, and stepped inside.

"Mako, follow Lucky. You'll be between the two of us."

"I'm not getting in there," she answered.

"You claustrophobic?" Shepherd asked.

"No," she said archly. "If I were, I would've lost it locked in the vault, right?"

"Right," he said in an easygoing tone.

"The dark?"

"I heard a sound."

"They're more afraid of you than you are of them," Colton Darcy said.

"Says the man who grew up in America," Mako said.

"What's that mean?"

"You coming or what?" Lucky's voice sounded strained.

"Stand by," Shepherd called to her before turning to Mako. "If you can't go in the tunnel, I'll stay here to protect you," he said. "But I'm almost out of ammo. I'm a pretty optimistic guy and I've lived more than nine lives, but if we stay right now, we're basically signing our death warrant."

"It's a phobia." She let out a long sigh. "I know it's stupid."

"You got this," he said. "Uncle Max needs you. How is he supposed to fix all the evil in the world without you?"

"I'm not getting in that tunnel."

"There's another way to the village," Colton Darcy said. "We can go out the back access door and into the woods."

"It's more dangerous," Shepherd said. "But it might work."

"We can leave tracks. Be a decoy. We'll stagger our prints and double back so it looks like the whole group went that way," Mako said. "We'll cut into the woods and then cover our tracks when we leave the woods again at the village. They'll think we went deeper into the woods and that will lead them away from the village."

"I don't know. My job is to protect you," Shepherd said.

"I'm going AWOL."

"I got her, Shepherd," Colton said.

With a loud sigh, Shepherd said, "We'll meet you at the village."

Just then a shadow fell across the strip of light that filtered in through the hole in the wall. They heard voices speaking Russian.

Without a word, Mako and Colton began to run.

Shepherd stepped into the tunnel and silently closed the door behind him.

33

Tiberius and his men stepped out the back door of the compound.

The wind had settled, but snow was still swirling and visibility was limited to half a football field.

Tiberius squinted into the distance. A low cloud cover hung in the sky. It was slightly orange, reflecting the light of the closest village.

"They must be headed that way." He pointed straight ahead.

"I don't know." One of his men crouched down. "Look."

Footprints in the snow led toward a wooded area to their left.

"Unleash the wolves," Tiberius said. "They will get to them faster than we can."

"No," the wolf handler said in a calm tone.

Tiberius whirled.

That's when he realized the wolves were no longer at his side but flanking their handler.

"What?" Tiberius said, a confused, furious look crossing his face. "You do as I say, just like they do as I say."

"Not today," the wolf handler said.

"You dare argue with me?"

"I'm not releasing my wolves on women and children."

Tiberius made a clicking sound but the wolves merely raised their heads to look at him. Sputtering with anger, Tiberius raised the whistle to his lips and blew it. The wolves pricked their ears but then looked up at the handler, who gave the slightest shake of his head.

"What?" Tiberius said. "This is treason."

"It would be if you were a king," the wolf handler said matter-of-factly. "But you are not a king."

"I am the alpha."

"Are you?" the handler said in a calm voice.

Tiberius clenched his fists, and as his face grew red, he stepped toward the wolf handler. The wolves growled.

The handler cocked his head and gave a wry smile.

"You're a dead man," Tiberius said. He turned to his motley crew of remaining soldiers. "Kill him!"

"If I give the command, my wolves will kill you. So yes, I will be dead, but so will you."

Tiberius scowled. "Your wolves?"

"You heard me."

For a second, Tiberius stood, face red and sweaty, hands clenched into fists at his side. His eyes narrowed.

"Keep those animals in check or I'll put them down—along with you—when all this is over."

Then he turned and began to follow the set of prints in the snow.

34

Shepherd quickly caught up with the others in the tunnel.

"Everything good?" Lucky asked him in a low voice.

"Mako and Colton are going to be decoys. They're going out the back door of the compound. They'll leave clear tracks in the snow but the tracks will lead into the woods. Then they'll cut over and meet us at the village."

"Their funeral," Lucky responded.

"It smells bad," Cassidy said. "I'm going to puke."

"It's just been closed up for ten years, honey. That's what you smell."

Will let out a blood-curdling scream and shouted, "Something touched my foot! It moved. It was alive."

"Shhh," Elizabeth Brody said.

"It's fine, Liz," Pete said. "Unless they're in the tunnel behind us, nobody can hear a thing. We're deep underground."

"Great," Cassidy said.

"Damn it!" Elizabeth yelled. "I think I twisted my ankle."

"I'll help you." Lucky reached for her in the dark, looping an arm around the other woman's waist.

"It's fine," Elizabeth said. "I think I'm okay now. Thanks."

Then the party began walking again in the cold, dark, damp tunnel.

After about ten minutes, Pete let out a loud exclamation.

"Pete?" Liz said. "Are you okay?"

"It can't be," he wailed.

"What is it?" Shepherd shouted.

"A dead end," Pete said, his voice full of despair. "We've hit a brick wall. It doesn't make any sense. We should be at the village by now."

One of the kids started to cry. Soft sniffing and sobbing sounds filled the tunnel.

"Shhh," Elizabeth said. "It's okay. We'll figure something out."

"There's got to be a way out," Pete said. "The plans showed an access point to the village. They wouldn't just build the tunnel and stop before they got to the village. That doesn't make any sense."

"Dad?" Cassidy said.

Elizabeth shushed her. "Just let your dad think for a second."

"I feel cold air," Pete said. "Everybody start feeling the walls. Maybe there's a panel or something I missed."

"Dad?" Cassidy said again. Everyone ignored her as they all reached for the surrounding walls and reported back.

"I don't feel anything."

"Nothing."

"Nope."

"Okay, okay. That's fine," he responded in a low voice, almost as if he was talking to himself.

"Think, think, think!" he said. "If only I had the blueprints they would give me a clue."

"Dad?" Cassidy again.

"What, champ?" he finally said.

"Look up."

They all lifted their heads.

There was a lighter black. A gray.

"What? That's it!" Pete exclaimed. "There is a well on the blueprints next to the tunnel exit! Brilliant, Cassidy! That's how they would get the fresh water. With a well! Why didn't I think of that?"

Then everyone grew silent.

"How far up to the surface?" Elizabeth asked, voicing the question the rest of them had.

"I don't know," Pete answered in a soft voice. "I don't know."

"I got this," Lucky said.

"You sure?" Shepherd asked.

"I can scale this baby with my hands tied behind my back."

"Let me give you a lift, at least," he said.

Shepherd lifted Lucky onto his shoulders. She reached for the sides of the well.

"This will work," she said. "It's a little slippery, so just in case maybe stand back a ways into the tunnel."

"Why?" Will asked.

"In case she falls on us, dummy," Cassidy answered.

"Please don't fall, Lucky," he said.

"I won't," she said. "Stand by and I'll give you a report once I get to the surface. Maybe I'll find another entrance from up there."

In the dark, they could hear her scrabbling for a foothold.

"Watch out!" she shouted, and bits of dirt and debris tumbled to the bottom.

"Lucky?" Shepherd called.

"I'm good. I'm getting closer to the surface. The light is getting brighter." She sounded strained.

It was quiet for a few seconds.

"I'm there. Stand by."

Then the dark silhouette disappeared, replaced by a circle of light at the top.

"What's that light?" Will asked.

"I think that might be dawn breaking," Elizabeth said. "It's almost morning."

"Thank God," Cassidy said.

"Lucky?" Shepherd shouted.

Nothing.

They all waited, dread permeating the small space.

"We're going to die down here," Will said.

Just then a silhouette blocked out the circle of light.

"Watch out below!" Lucky called.

Everyone stood back.

A rope with a bucket at the end clattered down the sides of the well.

"Pete," Shepherd said. "I think I need to go up first to help Lucky pull you all up. If I use the rope to get to the surface, will you be able to send your family up one by one?"

"Yeah," Pete said. "I got it taken care of down here."

Then Shepherd grabbed the rope and began to climb.

Five minutes later, the bucket came back down.

"You first, sport," Pete said. He wrapped the rope around his son's waist and then had him step into the bucket. "Hold here." He placed his son's hands on the rope one on top of the other.

"Okay," Will said.

"Ready!" Pete called, and then the bucket was raised.

A few moments later, the bucket came down again.

"Liz, why don't you go so we have a parent up there," Pete said. There was something in his voice that made Cassidy start to cry.

"What if they're up there too, Daddy?"

He didn't answer, just secured Elizabeth and shouted, "Ready."

"You're next," he said to Cassidy.

"I'm still afraid of heights, you know."

"I know," he said in a calm voice. "But just think of it this way— you're actually not up in the air at all. Up there is the ground, so there are really no heights to be afraid of."

"Very funny," she said. "That's not helping."

But his words had distracted her while he wrapped the rope around her waist.

"Okay. Stand here. Hold on here. You'll be up there in less than two minutes." Before she could answer, he yelled, "Ready."

Ten minutes later, Pete Brody crawled out of the well, the last to emerge.

Shepherd and Lucky greeted him with their fingers to their lips and pointed.

The others stood in the shadows under a clump of trees.

He looked around. The morning light was growing stronger, and a few yards away, the village was starting to take shape in the dawn light.

35

The dim light of the sun rising to the east was blotted out by a canopy of dark clouds that settled over the village, turning the day as dark as night and dropping temperatures dramatically.

Snow flurries made it difficult to see more than a few feet in front of them as the group edged toward the houses.

As they walked, Shepherd and Lucky peered into the windows of several houses only to see thick layers of dust over everything. Only a few houses looked occupied, their small windows lit up in a golden glow.

Shepherd stopped at a house on the periphery of the village near another set of woods. Smoke rose from a small chimney, and behind the curtains, the windows held a warm glow.

"I want you to knock on the door and hide in this house," he said to Elizabeth. "That way we also have an escape route into the woods if you need it while I go find Courtney Mako. Lucky will stay here to protect you."

Elizabeth raised her fist to knock, and a few moments later, a petite woman with a wrinkled face, gray bun, and tattered shawl opened the door. She frowned when she saw the Brody family standing there shivering with snow whipping around them.

The woman eyed them warily for a few seconds. Then, without a word, she stepped back and gestured for them to enter.

Shepherd put his hands together and gave a slight bow, which the woman acknowledged with a dip of her head.

Lucky filed in after the family and the woman waited a second for Shepherd to come, but he shook his head and she closed the door.

He immediately turned in the direction of the Cryer compound.

The blowing snow was blinding so he held up his forearm to block it as he forged a path through the blizzard. He heard a sound to his right where the woods lay and whirled, reaching for his weapon.

He was about to duck when he saw Colton Darcy and Courtney Mako.

They were covered in snow. Mako's cheeks were red and her head white with a light covering of snow. Colton's eyebrows and mustache were frosted white with ice and snow. Mako began to give Shepherd a grim smile, her hand half raised, when a rifle shot rang out.

Colton fell to the ground. Crimson blood quickly spread, staining the snow in front of him. Mako screamed and threw herself on the ground partly behind his body.

Shepherd turned in time to see a rebel fighter pivot his rifle in his direction.

Instinctively Shepherd ducked for cover behind a nearby house. Bullets peppered the side of the house where he'd been standing. He crouched low and grabbed a mirror out of his rucksack. Holding it out and around the corner of the house, he squinted to watch the shooter. He wanted to make sure they were ignoring Mako and Colton's body and concentrating on coming after him. He wanted Mako to have a shot at running for the cover of the woods.

The reflection showed a line of fighters racing through the swirling snow to take cover behind a house situated kitty-corner to his hideout. He watched as they conferred, and then the front soldier, leading with his gun, walked toward the edge of the house, ready to fire.

Shepherd stood and stepped out into the open, gun held before him.

As soon as the soldier peeked around the house, Shepherd fired, sending him scuttling back.

Another soldier appeared, this one closer. He raised his gun to shoot Shepherd. Before he could pull the trigger, two gunshots rang out, and his body jerked as he fell back to the ground.

Shepherd snapped his head to the right and saw in surprise that Courtney Mako stood over Colton's body, holding a gun with both hands. Her arms were extended in front of her and her entire body was shaking.

In the silence of the falling snow, there was a crackling sound. Mako's eyes widened and she looked down at her wrist. She gave a small smile, and Shepherd smiled back as she held up her wrist and spoke.

Shepherd shook his head in wonder. Her wrist comm was working. Being in the vault must have protected it from the EMP pulse.

"Run!" Shepherd shouted. "I'll cover for you."

Slowly she turned to meet his eyes. He stepped out further and fired sporadically at the edge of the house where he'd spotted the remaining soldiers.

No response.

As Mako backed away, dragging Colton's body, Shepherd turned to fire at the soldiers again to make sure they stayed put.

Before he ducked behind the house, he turned to make sure Mako had been able to take cover. He caught a last glimpse of her dragging Colton by his feet before she disappeared into the woods.

A few seconds later, he heard Tiberius's booming voice.

The drug warlord had arrived.

36

Back at the house in the village, Pete and Lucky exchanged a look when they heard the gunfire.

Elizabeth Brody was trying to speak broken Russian to the elderly woman, who did not seem startled or unduly concerned by the sound of gunfire.

"I better go see what's happening," Lucky said, taking a step toward the door.

Pete followed her as she stepped outside.

"You're outnumbered," he said. "Give me a gun. Let me help. Tell me what to do. I'm in this with you guys. You saved my family. Let me help save you."

"Thanks, but they'd pick you off in a second," Lucky said. "These are hardened assassins."

"You need a distraction? I'll run. I'll take off that way. I'm a really fast runner. I had a scholarship for track in college."

"You can't outrun a bullet," Lucky said. "These are bad dudes. Former Special Forces Spetsnaz Russian soldiers, I'd bet."

"There has to be something I can do?" he asked.

Lucky nodded. "There is. Protect your family. I hate to abandon you. You have an important job to keep everyone here safe."

"We'll be fine. They need you, Lucky," he said. "You need to go."

Just then, they heard a voice boom, "The diamond. Give me the diamond or we will hunt everyone down and feed them to the wolves."

"Tiberius," Lucky said. "He's close. Really close. You need to get inside. Now! Turn out all the lights, lock the door, put out the fire, and take cover in a back room. We'll come get you when it's clear. If you haven't heard from us by tomorrow, you should try to radio for help. Search every house until you find a way to call for help."

Then she was gone.

Pete nodded grimly and stepped back into the warm house.

"Cassidy, kill the lights. Elizabeth, lock the door. I'm going to put out the fire. Then we all go to the back room. Let's go!"

"What about me, Dad?" Will asked.

"Grab those pokers from the stand in front of the fireplace."

Will's eyes grew huge and he smiled.

Once everything was done, Pete herded his family and the older woman into a back bedroom. They closed and barricaded the door with a dresser.

He turned to Will, who stood clutching two fireplace pokers.

"Thanks, sport," he said, and took them both before handing one to Liz.

"I wish we had something else," she said in a low voice.

He turned toward the woman. "Do you have a gun?"

"I hardly think she would have a gun," Liz said.

"Maybe for hunting?"

The woman looked at him blankly. He held his fingers up, pointed them like a gun, and fired toward the door. Then he looked at her.

She shook her head.

"Okay, no gun. That's fine. Just lay low here."

A volley of gunfire rang out. The clear sound of a woman screaming seemed to echo through the village.

Pete stood and pushed the dresser aside.

"Where are you going?" Cassidy's voice was frantic. "Dad, you can't leave us here alone."

Tears streamed down her face.

"I need to help them distract the soldiers so we can get the others in here with us."

"Why are they still coming after us?" she said. "I don't understand."

Pete scratched his head. "I'm not sure. The leader, Tiberius, was shouting something about a diamond. I have no idea what he's talking about."

Will's face suddenly drained of color.

"You okay, kiddo?" Pete asked. "I'm not going to let him get to you."

"I know what they want," he said, his voice calm and firm.

"You do?" Elizabeth moved toward her son.

"Yeah." He nodded.

"What is it, son?" Pete crouched down before him.

The boy blew out a big puff of air and then looked at his sister.

"Don't look at me," she said shrilly. "I don't know what's going on."

Will reached into his jacket and took out a drawstring bag.

"I picked this up by the helicopter," Will said. "One of the bad guys saw me. It's my fault they are coming after us."

"What is it, son?" Pete asked.

Will slowly, painstakingly untied the cord and pulled open the bag. Then he stuck his hand in the pouch. He withdrew a closed fist and then opened it, his palm flat.

A massive diamond was nestled in his hand.

"Oh my God," Cassidy said. "Is that thing even real?"

Elizabeth's eyes grew wide as she looked at Pete.

"If this is what he wants, let's give it to him," Pete said.

"You can't just give it to him," Liz said.

"I can. I can give him the diamond and then he'll leave us alone." He reached for the diamond.

For a second, his son closed his fingers around the gem.

"Will?"

Will swallowed. "Dad. Give it to Mr. Shepherd. Let him give it to that guy. Or me. It's my fault they are after us."

"That's not true," Pete said. "They would come after us no matter what. But you might have the answer. Maybe if we give him this, he'll go and leave us alone. Can you give it to me now?"

Will stared for a long second and then opened his palm.

Pete plucked the diamond out and stuck it back in the pouch. He tied the cords in a loose knot and then tucked the entire satchel into the large pocket of his down coat.

"Pete?" Elizabeth said. "You don't have to do this."

"Listen," he said, and crouched down before his family. "I have to do this. It's the only way. That guy is not going away until he has this diamond."

"Will is right," Liz said. "One of the others can give him the diamond."

"They can't." Pete shook his head. "They are outgunned already. They need to be able to shoot if necessary. I need to be the one to offer up the diamond."

"Daddy!" Cassidy said. "They're just going to shoot you and take it. Why would they let you live if they know you have it."

Pete frowned. "I'm not going to let that happen."

But he gave his wife a look over his children's heads. She bit her lip hard to keep from crying.

"I'll be back. Wait here. Don't move until I come get you, okay?"

They nodded.

He reached for Will and wrapped him in a huge hug.

"I love you, buddy. You take care of your mom and sister, okay? You were really smart to pick up this diamond. It's what's going to save us."

"Or get Dad killed," Cassidy sobbed.

Pete took her hands, wiping a tear away. "Take care of your mother and brother. I love you."

Then he stood and held his wife in his arms.

"I love you, Liz."

"I'm proud of you, Pete," she said. "You're a wonderful husband and father. I don't tell you that enough."

He smiled grimly and then reached for the door handle.

The kids ran to Elizabeth and they huddled on the bed, holding each other and crying as Pete stepped out of the room.

Pete Brody peeked out the front window of the cottage. When he saw it was clear, he quickly stepped outside, closing the door behind him, and ran toward the sound of gunfire.

He whipped around the corner of a house and was immediately tackled to the ground. He began to flail and fight. A hand was over his mouth. Then he saw Lucky's face above him. She held a finger to her lips. He nodded and she removed her hand. Then she turned and gestured for him to follow her on all fours.

They crawled behind a stack of wood and a small shed toward the other side of the house. Then she stood and pulled him up with her.

Shepherd stood there, gun raised by his head, back flat against the house. He nodded when he saw Pete.

"What are you doing here?" Lucky hissed.

Before Pete could answer, Shepherd spoke in a low voice.

"They've got Courtney Mako pinned in the woods. We need to rescue her. It could get hairy. Why don't you go back to your family and we'll find you later."

"They won't just give up," Pete whispered back. "You heard him. He's after the diamond."

"If that thing was in the helicopter that crashed, it's lost forever," Lucky said. "He's delirious."

"Is he?" Pete raised an eyebrow.

"Spill it," Shepherd said.

"The diamond that Tiberius is looking for..." Pete patted the front of his coat. "I got it."

Lucky squinted at him and tilted her head.

Shepherd held out his hand.

Pete shook his head. "You need to provide cover for me while I go meet Tiberius. We meet in the middle. I hand him the diamond. They leave. We leave. End of story."

"If only it could be that simple," Lucky said.

"Can't it?" he asked.

"It rarely is," Shepherd said. He looked at Lucky, and she nodded.

Backing around to the opposite side of the shed, she ducked behind an adjacent house where Pete could still see her, then shouted,

"Tiberius. We have the diamond. Let our men go and we'll give it to you."

There was silence for a few seconds.

Shepherd peeked his head around the corner.

"They're talking."

After a few seconds, a man's voice responded.

"We all step into the clearing. Nobody shoots. If anyone shoots, there will be no exchange; there will only be a massacre."

"Agreed," Shepherd shouted.

"On ten," Lucky said, and began to count.

As Lucky and Shepherd stepped out from the building, four rebel fighters stepped into the clearing.

Everyone held out their weapons warily.

"Outgunned again," Lucky said under her breath to Shepherd.

"Story of our life," he said.

The six eyed each other warily.

"Send the diamond to the middle," a man yelled.

"Where is Tiberius?" Shepherd yelled back.

Tiberius stepped out from behind the building.

Two massive wolves flanked him, pressing close to his thighs.

"If I go down," Tiberius said, "my wolves will kill your man instantly."

"Understood," Lucky said.

Shepherd whispered, "Who is the guy behind him? The skinny guy with the long hair and beard?"

"I don't know, but I saw him give the wolves something to eat right before they stepped out," she said.

"I am not a patient man," Tiberius said. "Let's do this now."

Lucky nodded, and Pete stepped out from the cover of the building.

He held the satchel in his hands.

Shepherd grunted.

"What is it?" Lucky asked.

"Where are the rest of his men?"

Lucky swung her head around, searching. "How many are we missing?"

"Based on the positions where we were under fire, I'd say we're missing at least two if not more."

Lucky stepped forward. "Any funny business with your men trying to ambush us, I'll go down with you, Tiberius. I'll die willingly if it means you die as well. Don't forget that."

The rebel warlord scowled. "We walk now," he said.

"Go," Shepherd said to Pete.

"Wait," Lucky said. "Pete, you're absolutely one hundred percent sure this is what you want? You can still turn back. I'll walk the diamond over there. I wouldn't mind being within teeth-kicking range of this jackhole."

Pete looked determined. His lips were pressed tightly together and his eyes were narrowed. "I have to do this," he said. "I dragged my family over here to this country and put their lives in danger. It's up to me to end this or I won't be able to live with myself."

"Go, then," she said.

Slowly, warily, Tiberius and Pete each stepped toward the center of the clearing.

"You're a brave man," Tiberius said to Pete. "If you plan anything to trick me, you will pay with your life. Many people have tried to barter with that diamond. They're all dead."

"I don't want your blood diamond," Pete said with a sneer. "I want you to leave me and my family alone."

They were within ten feet of each other when there was a sound off to the right near a row of houses.

Shepherd whirled. Lucky kept her sights on the gun she had trained on Tiberius.

"Jesus," Shepherd said.

"What?" Lucky asked.

Then Pete's head swiveled and he let out a desperate wail. "No!"

"They've got the kid," Shepherd shouted.

"Put your guns down now." It was Tiberius.

"Bloody hell," Lucky said.

"And," Shepherd added, "the rest of his family is behind them."

The rebel warlord reached down into his shirt.

"Damn it," Lucky said. "He's reaching for something. A gun? Should I take my shot?"

"They'll kill those kids before his body hits the ground," Shepherd said.

"I'm going around to the back of them," Lucky said.

"Wait!" Shepherd said. "They'll pick you off. It's too dangerous."

But then she was gone.

Keeping his eye on his family, Pete dumped the diamond out of the satchel and into his palm.

"What are you doing?" Tiberius roared.

"Let my son go or I'll throw this diamond into the snow and you'll never find it," Pete said, holding the diamond aloft. "I had a scholarship in college for baseball. I played left field. I can throw this into the woods and it will be lost forever."

"Your son will be dead before you raise your arm," Tiberius said. "And your family."

As he spoke, Tiberius kept rummaging around inside his jacket and underneath the wolf skin as if he was searching for something. His movements were becoming more frantic.

The warlord swore.

"I told you," the skinny man behind him said. "I don't condone killing women and children."

Tiberius whirled. "You don't count," he said. "You do as I say—"

His words cut off as the wolf handler held up a hammered silver whistle.

"Looking for this?" the man said.

A red flush spread across Tiberius's cheeks. Then his eyes narrowed.

"You will pay for humiliating me like this," he said.

He reached beneath his wolf skin and withdrew a pistol.

He was about to raise it toward the wolf handler when the wolves at his side began to growl. They had their eyes trained on the handler. They were snapping and snarling and gnashing their teeth.

Tiberius smiled. "Even your precious wolves want to see you dead."

The wolf handler smiled too. "You pull that trigger and the wolves will be feasting on your intestines before my body hits the ground."

Tiberius looked down, and horror spread across his face. The wolves had backed up and were now snarling at him, their teeth flashing, drool dripping, jaws snapping.

With a loud shout, Lucky emerged from behind a house and shot the man who had been holding a gun on Will. Too late, Lucky realized another fighter was hiding behind her. She felt cold steel on the back of her neck and closed her eyes. Then a shot rang out and the pressure of the metal was gone.

She whirled to see the man fall dead behind her.

Across from him, Mako stood, her arms outstretched and her gun still pointing at where the man had been. Lucky gave her a nod, and Mako's mouth spread into a small smile. She mouthed, "One for me."

Then both women turned and began shooting at the other fighters.

In the chaos, Tiberius raised his own gun and aimed it at the wolf handler.

True to his prediction, before the man's body hit the snow in a pool of blood, the wolves were on Tiberius. His outraged roar quickly turned to howls of agony as the wolves pounced and took him to the ground, tearing at his face and neck. Arterial blood from a jagged incision at his neck sprayed in a large arc as the wolves tugged at his flesh.

Soon, all but one fighter remained.

Lucky raised her arm to shoot but he fell forward, his chest blossoming red.

"What the?" Shepherd said.

"Darcy," Lucky said, and pointed. "The guardian angel with nine lives."

Colton Darcy was lying prone at the base of the woods, a sniper rifle in his outstretched arms propped on a fallen log.

Lucky turned and saw Pete Brody on his knees in the snow, clutching his family to him. All four of them had tears running down their cheeks. Around them the snow was soaked with blood and dead bodies, but they were crying and smiling, oblivious to everything but each other.

"Look," Shepherd said, pointing.

Villagers began to pour into the clearing. They all stood at the edge, staring at Tiberius's body as the wolves feasted.

One of them, an older man with a wobbly chin, spotted Tiberius on the ground. As the rest watched, he walked over to the warlord's body.

"Watch out!" Lucky yelled.

But the man kept walking until he stood right above the body. The wolves looked up at him but seemed unconcerned and kept eating. The man looked down at Tiberius and nodded. Then he turned and walked away with a gap-toothed smile. The rest of the villagers began to cheer.

Lucky was about to walk over to greet them when a loud rumble froze her in her tracks. Everybody turned toward the path leading toward the Cryer compound. The ground shook as the noises grew louder. Within seconds, two massive orange snowcats came roaring into the clearing.

They came to a stop. People exchanged anxious glances until the engines were turned off.

Shepherd smiled when he saw Red descend from the driver's seat of one of the vehicles. He was dressed in a camouflage snow suit that zipped up the front and wore a matching hat with fur-lined ear flaps.

"It's about time," Mako said. "I called him an hour ago from my wrist comm."

"An hour?" Shepherd said. "What did he do to get here so quickly? Teleport? I think that's pretty good."

Mako rolled her eyes. "Pretty good, huh? I think pretty good would have been six hours ago when I first called."

"I heard you needed me to bring in the big guns," Red said, and slapped hands with Shepherd. Two men holding first-aid kits stood beside him.

"Very funny."

When everyone turned, they saw that the wolves had disappeared. But not before they'd gnawed off Tiberius's face.

"Who's the handsome fella?" Red asked.

"Guess," Lucky said.

"A fitting end." Red turned to look at the carnage around them. "I'd say you did fine without me. I don't think there's anyone on the other side who needs any medical attention. Not anymore."

"That man over there needs some." Lucky pointed at Colton Darcy, who was still propped up on the log. "He's with us."

Colton brought his fingers together in a salute against his forehead. Red nodded and the man with the first-aid kit ran over.

Stepping forward, Shepherd squinted at the sky.

"It's clearing up. We have to get back to the border right away. This area isn't safe yet. Not for a while."

"He's right," Lucky said. "Another rebel group is just waiting in the wings to step forward. We can come back later with more manpower to secure the compound and village, but for now we need to leave."

"If you want to come back here, you're on your own," Colton piped up from the ground where a medic was examining him.

Cassidy Brody laughed.

Red mumbled something. Lucky looked at him and raised an eyebrow. He pointed to his earbud, held up his wrist with the comm, and mouthed, "Max."

Lucky nodded.

"Okay, Max," Red said. "We are clearing out. We can fit our entire crew in the snowcats and will head straight to the border. It might take us an hour. We'll see you on the plane."

Then he turned toward Pete Brody.

"Max owns the entire company outright now. Mako told him that you had some plans for the factory. He wants to know if you have time to meet with him and talk about your plans to bring fresh water to the village?"

Pete looked around, and his wife smiled and nudged him. "Answer him, Pete."

"Yeah! Yeah, I do!"

Pete cleared his throat, then looked at the villagers before gazing down at the diamond still in his hand.

"With all due respect," he said to Red. "I think this diamond could do a lot of good here."

Mako was beside him now. "I agree with Mr. Brody. A diamond with that much blood on it could do a lot of good to help these people."

"What do you have in mind?" Pete asked. "It's a blood diamond. Probably half the world will want it once they learn of its existence. We can't just sell it at auction. It has to be authenticated ... it has to be..."

Liz put her hand on her husband's forearm. He closed his mouth.

Mako smiled. "You mean someone who is very powerful and knows how to work under the radar needs to get ahold of the diamond and make sure it's used for good, not bad?"

"Yes," Pete said. "Exactly."

"Great. I know just the person."

"You do?"

"Yep." She winked. "You're meeting with him later."

37

When the private jet touched down at London's Heathrow Airport, Will and Cassidy were the only ones wide awake.

Cassidy had spent the entire flight taking pictures of the inside of the jet, filming herself bouncing on the huge queen bed in the bedroom, and editing everything to post on social media.

Because the jet had WIFI, she also went live a few times, giving dramatically voiced tours of the jet. She went seat to seat and introduced everyone except Lucky, Shepherd, and Red, who said they had to stay anonymous. She used a filter that made their faces clowns.

"Perfect," Red said when he saw it.

Will was busy playing video games on the jet's high-tech system using the big-screen TV.

Since they were the only ones awake when the pilot announced their descent, they figured they didn't even need to sit down and put their seatbelts on. There wasn't an adult to tell them otherwise, since a curtain separated them from the stewards at the back of the plane. Instead, they pretended they were surfing with their legs spread wide as they tried to keep their balance for the landing.

By the time Pete and Liz opened their eyes, their children were giggling wildly and had finally sat down.

As the plane landed, Pete reached over to squeeze his wife's hand.

"It's so good to see them laugh," she said.

"Doesn't mean they still won't need therapy," he said.

Liz gave a long sigh. "I know. But they are remarkably strong."

Everyone stood to get off the plane.

"They'll be just fine," said Red, who was standing nearby. "They've got you two for parents."

"I've got a question for you," Lucky said as she hoisted her backpack on.

"Oh, yeah?" Pete answered.

"I've been wondering about something you said. Did you say that you had scholarships for both track and baseball in college?"

Pete burst out laughing. "Well, I only had one for track. I was bluffing about the baseball one."

Liz opened her mouth wide. "You lied? I don't know if I've ever caught you in a lie!"

"Well, it *was* to save our son's life."

"Fair enough," she said with a smile.

After a few moments of silence, Pete cleared his throat.

"Guess this is where we all peel off and part ways," he said.

"You guys going straight back to the States?" Shepherd asked, and then yawned.

Pete and Liz exchanged a look.

"Not sure," he said.

"Here's the thing," Liz said. "We don't have a house. We don't really have anything. We sold it all. We paid for our flights over because we were told we'd be reimbursed, but…"

"With Cryer dead, you're worried about all that?" Red asked.

She nodded.

Mako piped up. "Worry about nothing. It will all be handled," she said crisply.

The steward had opened the jet door and people began to walk forward.

"When you get to the tarmac, please go to the large van," the steward said. "It will take you to your private lounge."

Liz raised an eyebrow and Cassidy smiled. "This is so cool."

The van drove them to another part of the airport and let them out in front of a small private door. Another man in a white uniform held it open. It led to a small set of stairs going up.

At the top was a large room with a buffet, tables, leather couches, and a big-screen TV. Two doors led to bathrooms and four to bedrooms.

"Wow," Will said, reaching for one of the gaming controls on a coffee table.

"Wait, honey," Liz said.

"Max asked that we do our debriefing here," Mako said. "He has an announcement to make and then we will show the Brody family to their hotel. You three are sleeping here and catching the next flight to the States in the morning."

"What about us?" Cassidy whispered to her mom.

Her mother held up a hand.

"Please grab some food and be seated," a man in a white uniform said.

Once everyone had a plate full of food, they sat eating and facing the big-screen TV.

A news station was broadcasting breaking news.

"Look, Dad," Will said. "The reporter said that pirates took over that boat. I didn't think there were pirates anymore. Like, isn't that just cartoon stuff, like Jack Sparrow and Peter Pan?"

"No, dummy," Cassidy said.

"There actually are pirates, sport," Pete said. "Modern pirates board cargo, tanker, and container ships, mostly. They usually look for a safe with cash and then rob all the people onboard the ship. But every once in a while they will hold the crew and ship itself hostage if the ship is carrying something valuable and demand a ransom. That's more rare, though. Usually they board, grab all the valuables, and then leave."

"Cool," Will said.

"Not cool—" Pete's words cut off as the TV screen went white and then crackled to life again.

"Good work, everyone," a voice said, and then a man appeared. He was standing on what looked like a Western-style porch. He was a tall, slim, handsome Indian man with shoulder-length wavy hair and smiling eyes.

"Hey," Pete said. "Your name isn't Max, it's—"

"Maximilian," Liz Brody said, smoothly cutting her husband off before he could say he recognized the famous tech billionaire Jay Ravi.

"I'm terribly sorry that your family was caught up in this disaster, Mr. Brody," Max began. "When I sent Mako to investigate, we thought there might be a little fraud going on. We had no idea the extent of Mr. Cryer's monstrosities. I am deeply ashamed that my money played a part in this. I have so much damage to undo. It will take years for me to right the wrongs that Mr. Cryer has done. So I'm going to need help. I'm going to need someone I can trust. I'm going to need someone to take over the company."

Max paused.

"I'm asking you, no, I'm begging you, Mr. Brody, to accept the company as your own. It will be called Brody Plastics. It will not be easy for you to turn it around, but I know you have the ability to make it a recycling plant that not only brings the village fresh water and helps them rebuild but also sets an example to others doing business in this destabilized region. I will make sure security matches that of Fort Knox if you choose to accept."

Pete Brody's face was bright red.

"Mr. Max, sir," he said. "I'm greatly honored and I know I could do the job up to your standards, but I don't know if my family would want to go back there..."

He trailed off.

"We would only ask you to fly out there once a month for a week to oversee operations. You would handpick your team from the best in the world to run the place while you aren't there," Max said. "Does that help?"

Pete looked at his family. Liz nodded and smiled. Will nodded. Cassidy looked at the rest of her family and then shrugged.

"We're in!" Pete said.

"Excellent," Max said. "I'm going to have you stay one night in

London while we figure out just what city you want to live in when you get back to the States. The company is buying you a home. Be picky. You can live anywhere."

After hugs and tearful goodbyes, the Brody family was led out of the private lounge by a man in a suit.

EPILOGUE

After the door closed, Lucky stood in front of the TV screen with her hands on her hips.

"What about us?" she asked. "What's next?"

Uncle Max laughed. "You afraid you're going to get bored?"

"Nah," she said. "I'm just curious."

"Go home first. Get some R&R and then we'll talk about your next assignment."

"That sounds great, but, uh, we don't really have a home anymore," Shepherd said.

"Sir?" Colton Darcy asked.

"Yes, Mr. Darcy."

"After I was shot and Mako dragged me into the woods, she said something to me about you, but I'm sort of wondering if I imagined it or made it up in my delirium?"

"Oh, yeah. Shoot. I'm so sorry. I forgot you haven't actually agreed yet. I was assuming you would. My fault. Colton Darcy, I'd love to have you be part of my team. You are a good man and worked well with the fox and Shepherd."

"The fox?"

"Oh, sorry. Lucky."

Colton grinned at Lucky and then turned back to the screen.

"I'd love to work for you, Mr. Max."

"Well, then I'd like to invite you to your new home. Stand by."

The camera panned back and showed some mountains, horses, a few barns, and a huge house.

"What?" Lucky raised one well-shaped eyebrow. "Where is that?"

"Cryer left this ranch behind. It was actually bought by the company for its employees. It's your new home if you want it. All four of you. There are half a dozen huge separate living quarters and then common spaces. A little like a commune setup. You have your own wing of the place and then can share the living room, family room, theater, game room, kitchen, etc. I'm having the best of the best install the highest-tech security I can find on earth. It will be your safe place. Your haven, if you will."

"Like the Batcave?" Shepherd asked.

"Exactly," Max said.

"I'm only in if it's like Harley Quinn's lair," Lucky said.

Max burst into laughter.

Colton said, "No clue."

"It's an abandoned shopping mall," Shepherd said.

"Oh hell, I'm in if it's like the Batcave," Lucky said.

"So that's a yes for the fox and Shepherd," Max said. "Red?"

"You had me at the word ranch," he said. "I've always loved Montana and God knows I miss having horses."

"That leaves you, Darcy," Max said. "What do you think?"

"I'm an easy sale. I've been living in barracks. At least this joint has windows and probably better sheets. I'm in."

Everybody laughed.

"What about Mako?" Shepherd asked, looking at the petite woman.

She blushed. "Thank you for your concern, but I don't do rural. I'll stick to my city penthouse any day."

"That's all for now. Your flight to Billings leaves in the morning. A driver will be waiting."

Before they could answer and thank Max, he clicked off.

"Well, it's time for me to catch my flight," Mako said.

"Back to the States?" Shepherd asked.

"No." She smiled.

"So mysterious," he said, and grinned back.

He reached over and shook her hand. "Nice working with you."

"Oh, we'll see much more of each other. Just you wait."

She was about to leave when Lucky caught up.

"Hey," Lucky said.

Mako stopped and turned.

"I owe you. A life debt."

"You don't owe me anything," Mako said.

"I actually do." Lucky smiled. "And I also owe you a thank you."

"Well, I'll take the thank you. You're welcome. But I owe you for making sure we all got out of there safely."

"Until next time?" Lucky said.

Mako smiled. "Looking forward to it. I think between the two of us, we bring the perfect combination of brawn and brains. In equal measure," she said quickly.

Then, before Lucky could answer, Mako walked out the door.

"What was that about?" Shepherd asked.

"Nothing," Lucky said.

Then she stood back and eyed him.

"What?" he said, shifting uncomfortably.

Lucky laughed.

"Just trying to imagine how you are going to look in a pair of leather chaps."

THE MEMORY BANK
By Brian Shea and Raquel Byrnes

When a series of high-profile deaths is linked to a lethal conspiracy, Detective Morgan Reed must risk everything to uncover the truth.

Technology pioneer Dr. Gerard Price is at the height of his scientific career. After years of research in the field of memory augmentation, he's just made a world-changing breakthrough.

But his life's work is mysteriously cut short by a fatal overdose in a seedy motel.

All evidence points to a suicide, and the case is closed...until Detective Morgan Reed begins working a series of similarly strange deaths.

As Reed joins forces with Detective Natalie De La Cruz to expose the lies and corporate treachery at the heart of the suicides, they discover a shocking plot that will put thousands of lives at risk.

In a world where cutting-edge technology meets dirty money, Reed and De La Cruz must navigate the labyrinths of an impenetrable network to save countless innocents from certain death...as their own lives hang in the balance.

SHEA & BYRNES deliver an explosive techno-thriller that will keep you up all night—perfect for fans of Michael Crichton and David Baldacci.

Get your copy today at
severnriverbooks.com

ABOUT THE AUTHORS

Brian Shea has spent most of his adult life in service to his country and local community. He honorably served as an officer in the U.S. Navy. In his civilian life, he reached the rank of Detective and accrued over eleven years of law enforcement experience between Texas and Connecticut. Somewhere in the mix he spent five years as a fifth-grade school teacher. Brian's myriad of life experience is woven into the tapestry of each character's design. He resides in New England and is blessed with an amazing wife and three beautiful daughters.

USA TODAY bestselling and Agatha, Anthony, Barry, and Macavity Award Finalist Kristi Belcamino writes dark mysteries about fierce women seeking justice. She is a crime fiction writer, cops beat reporter, and Italian mama who also bakes a tasty biscotti. In her former life, as an award-winning crime reporter at newspapers in California, she flew over Big Sur in an FA-18 jet with the Blue Angels, raced a Dodge Viper at Laguna Seca, and attended barbecues at the morgue. Belcamino has written and reported about many high-profile cases including the Laci Peterson murder and Chandra Levy's disappearance. She has appeared on Inside Edition and her work has appeared in the *New York Times*, *Writer's Digest*, *Miami Herald*, *San Jose Mercury News*, and *Chicago Tribune*.

To find out more, visit
severnriverbooks.com

Printed in the United States
by Baker & Taylor Publisher Services